"A
sai

And Stephanie
were true.

"But you're the one in my arms. Why don't you satisfy me?" Brock challenged softly.

Stephanie's heart ran away with itself at the thought. Both his arms were around her, his fingers spread as they roamed over her shoulders, her back, slowly caressing and molding her to him, his virility a potent force that left her weak. Her head was tipped back, enabling her to look into his eyes. They were smiling at her, with an inner satisfaction and supreme confidence, the certainty of his ability to seduce her.

Stephanie supposed she was transparent; her pride was injured that she was such an easy conquest for him. But was there a woman born who could deny his attraction for long?

JANET DAILEY AMERICANA

Janet Dailey
Americana

HEART OF STONE

Harlequin Books

TORONTO • NEW YORK • LONDON
AMSTERDAM • PARIS • SYDNEY • HAMBURG
STOCKHOLM • ATHENS • TOKYO • MILAN

The state flower depicted on the cover of this book is purple lilac.

Janet Dailey Americana edition published August 1987
Second printing August 1988
Third printing August 1989

ISBN 373-21929-6

Harlequin Presents edition published November 1980

Original hardcover edition published in 1980
by Mills & Boon Limited

CHAPTER ONE

THERE WAS a sudden flurry of activity outside Stephanie's office. Located in the heart of the luxurious New Hampshire inn, it gave her ready access to all phases of the operation. Through the open doorway Stephanie had a partial view of the front desk, which gave her a feeling of the comings and goings of the guests. Across the hall was the housekeeping department. The office next to hers belonged to her brother, Perry Hall, the manager of the inn, and her boss.

When Mrs. Adamson, the dining-room hostess, went hurrying past Stephanie's door, her curiosity was throughly aroused. Something unusual was going on. Even though she had actually worked in the White Boar Inn a short three months,

Stephanie felt the accelerated tempo of the inn's pulse, a tense quickening of interest.

The unbalanced ledger sheet on her desk was forgotten as she speared the lead pencil through the chestnut hair above her ear and rose from her chair. Bookkeeping was invariably the last department to know anything if she allowed routine to run its normal course. Since Perry was her brother, she didn't choose to sit back and wait to be informed. She had been isolated from the mainstream of life for too many years to let it continue now that she had rejoined it.

In the hallway, she glanced toward the front desk. Her blue eyes noted the expressions of harried excitement in the faces of the usually unflappable pair manning the registration counter. It was rare indeed for the arrival of an important personage to create such a disturbance, since the inn catered to the wealthy and the notable. Besides, every room was already taken, occupied by guests on hand to view the autumn splendor of the White Mountains, and there were reservations all the way through the winter season to spring.

Puzzled by the unknown cause of all this barely subdued commotion, Stephanie absently fingered the scarab pendant suspended by a gold chain to nestle in the valley between her breasts, the loose weave of her white rollneck sweater providing a backdrop for the jewelry. The slight frown remained in her expression as she walked the few feet to her brother's office. The door was standing open and she paused within its frame, not wanting to interrupt her brother's consultation with Mrs. Adamson.

"Get a bottle on ice right away," he was instructing the woman, who was hastily making notes on a pad. Perry, too, was consulting the papers in front of him, not glancing up to see Stephanie in the doorway. His brown hair was rumpled as if he had run his fingers through it many times. "Fix a tray with a selection of cheeses and fresh fruits to go with it. You'd better recheck the wine cellar and make sure you have an ample supply of his favorite wines in stock, too. Alert your staff. I want them on their toes in case he decides to dine in the restaurant this evening. I don't want—Flowers!" Perry interrupted himself to exclaim. "I nearly forgot the damn flowers." He punched the buzzer to summon his secretary.

For once the young girl appeared within seconds. She looked pale and anxious, more timid than usual. Despite her youth, Connie York was highly skilled and competent. Her chief flaw was a marked lack of self-confidence, which was blatantly in evidence at the moment.

"Yes, Mr. Hall?" She made a question of her response to his summons, her small face pinched into tense lines of unease and framed with dark hair.

His upward glance took note of Stephanie in the doorway, but he didn't acknowledge her presence in his office beyond that. "Call the florist. If they can't have a bouquet of roses delivered here within ninety minutes, I want you to pick them up."

"Yes, sir." Her head bobbed in quick agreement, but she didn't make any move to follow through with the order.

Perry, who was usually extraordinarily patient with his self-effacing secretary, sent her an irritated look. "You aren't going to get it done standing there, Connie. Go on!"

"I know, but . . . ." She wavered uncertainly.

"What is it?" he demanded in short temper. "I haven't got time to coax it out of you."

Stephanie's gaze wandered over her brother's face in surprise. Six years older than herself, he rarely allowed stressful situations to shake him. He had been more than just her big brother: he had been her idol for as long as she could remember. Life hadn't been easy for him . . . or for her, either. Their mother had died when Stephanie was only four. Perry had played surrogate mother to her, fixing meals and keeping house while their father worked long hours, skilled only as a ski instructor and bartender, to make ends meet.

Five years ago, when Stephanie was seventeen, it had seemed the world would become their oyster. Perry had obtained a scholarship to attend a prestigious postgraduate law school and Stephanie had been accepted by a prominent women's college. Then a freak skiing accident had left their father a paraplegic, and Perry had given up his scholarship to take the position of assistant manager of this inn, while Stephanie stayed home to take care of their father. A virulent pneumonia virus had claimed their father four months ago. In many ways, his death had been a blessing— for him and for them.

Stephanie hadn't completely adjusted to the freedom from responsibility that had matured both of them beyond their years, while it deprived them of the pleasures of youth. The night course she had taken in accounting, to supplement their income by doing bookkeeping at home for small businesses, had provided her with the experience to take the post as bookkeeper at the inn when her predecessor had retired with a few grumblings about nepotism, because her brother had become the manager in the last year.

She liked working at the inn, being with people and being part of things. Most of all, she liked working with her brother. She had come to respect his competency in a position the duties of which were far ranging and varied. Perry always appeared to be totally in control whether dealing with a crisis in the restaurant kitchen or organizing the staff. Which was why Stephanie was surprised by his harried attitude at the moment. It didn't seem in character.

"It's just that . . . I was wondering . . . ." Connie was stumbling over the reason for her hesitation.

"I don't have all day. Please get to the point," Perry ordered.

"It's your appointment," his secretary began, intimidated by his abruptness.

"I told you to cancel them." His mouth thinned with impatience.

"Yes, but . . . ." She bit her lower lip.

Perry appeared to mentally count to ten in an effort to control his temper. "But what, Connie?" he asked with forced evenness.

"You're supposed to speak at a luncheon this noon." She rushed the explanation. "It's been on the agenda for two months. They couldn't possibly get anyone to take your place at such late notice."

Perry groaned. "Is that today?"

"Yes, sir." Anxiety tortured Connie's expression. "What should I do?"

"Do? There's nothing you can do," he sighed. "I'll have to attend the luncheon, but cancel everything else. And get those flowers."

"Yes, sir." With a nod of her head, the girl disappeared inside her adjoining office.

Returning his attention to the woman in front of his desk, Perry raked a hand through his dark hair again, adding to its disorder. "You know the routine, Mrs. Adamson. I trust you to handle it." He cast a glance at his wristwatch, in effect dismissing the hostess.

Stephanie stepped to one side so the woman could exit through the open door. From the conversation she had overheard, she had a general idea what was happening. With the exception of the private suite, the inn was fully booked. And the suite was reserved exclusively for the owner or his personal guests. Before she had a chance to ask whose arrival was anticipated, Perry was addressing her.

"Whatever your problem is, Stephanie, it will have to wait—unless someone has absconded with the receipts. In that case, I don't want to know about it for three days," he declared with a tired shake of his head.

"I don't have any problem," she assured him. "I'm just trying to figure out what's going on. Who's coming? The place is in a quiet uproar—if there is such a thing."

Sighing, Perry rocked back in his swivel chair. Eyes the same blue as her own, skimmed her slender figure in its white sweater and green tartan skirt. A faint smile touched his mouth when his gaze returned to her face with its soft frame of sleek chestnut hair.

"Brock is making another one of his impromptu visits. He called a half an hour ago to say he'd be here by two this afternoon. He's driving up from Boston," he explained, as tension etched lines in his strong face.

"Aha!" Stephanie mocked him to ease his concern. "Now I understand why everyone is jumping at the slightest sound. The big man himself is coming to inspect his property."

"It's all right for you to joke about it. Canfield expects the best and I am the one who has to explain why, if he doesn't get it." Perry rubbed his fingers against a spot in the center of his forehead.

"I don't know what you're worrying about." Stephanie walked to the back of his chair and let her hands knead the taut cords between his neck and shoulders. "Don't forget I've been keeping the books for the past three months. I know how very well the inn has been doing. Brock Canfield can't possibly have any complaints about your work or how you run the inn.''

''We have done well,'' he admitted, relaxing under the massage of her hands. ''If that trend continues through the winter ski season, we should have our best year ever.''

''That proves my point, doesn't it?'' she reasoned.

''The point will be proved only when it's accomplished,'' Perry reminded her. ''In the meantime, Brock is going to judge by what he sees on this trip.''

''He won't have any complaints.'' Stephanie was certain of that. The service at the inn was flawless. Even the hard-to-please guests found little to grumble about. ''Do you know this will be my first opportunity to meet this paragon of all manhood, Brock Canfield?'' she realized. ''You have worked here what? Five years? Everybody talks about him as if he was God. Depending on their sex, they either tremble or quiver when they hear his name.'' She laughed. ''I've heard him alternately described as a ruthless tycoon or a gorgeous hunk of man. Now I'll be able to find out for myself which is the real Brock Canfield!''

''He's both, plus a few other things.'' Her

brother took hold of one of her hands to end the rubdown and pull her around to the side of his chair. Handsome in an attractive kind of way, he studied her for a quiet second. "I have this luncheon to attend, so I'll have to deputize you to stand in for me in case I'm not back when Brock arrives."

"Me?" Stephanie frowned her surprise.

"Somebody has to be on hand to welcome him. Connie practically cringes every time he looks at her," Perry explained with a wry grimace. "And Vic is home sleeping after being on duty all night," he added, referring to the night manager. "I can't think of anyone else. Do you mind?"

"Of course not. What do I have to do, besides being on hand to greet him?" Despite her willing agreement, Stephanie experienced a shiver of unease at some of the more formidable descriptions she'd heard applied to the inn's owner.

"Show him to his suite and make certain everything is in order. Connie is getting the flowers and Mrs. Adamson will have a bottle of champagne on ice, along with some cheese and fruit. In general, just see that he has everything he wants."

"That sounds simple enough," she shrugged.

"Watch your step, Stephanie," her brother advised, suddenly serious.

She was confused by the warning. "I'm not likely to say anything that would offend him." She wasn't the outspoken type. Most of the time she was very tactful—able to curb her tongue despite the provocation.

"I know you wouldn't." He dismissed that possibility with a wave of his hand. "I was trying to say that you should stay clear of Brock Canfield. He goes through women the way a gambler goes through a deck of cards. He's rich, good-looking in a way, and can be both persuasive and forceful. I'm told that can be an irresistible combination."

"I've heard a few stories about him," Stephanie admitted.

"I wouldn't like to see you get mixed up with him, because I know you'd be hurt. Honestly, Steph, I'm not trying to play the heavy-handed big brother." Perry seemed to smile at himself. "It's just that I know he's going to take one look at you and get ideas. You haven't had all that much experience with men—especially his kind."

"Experienced or not, I think I can take care of myself." She didn't mind that Perry was worried about her. In fact, she liked the idea that he cared enough about her to try to protect her. A smile hovered around the corners of her mouth. "Is that why you never brought him home to dinner when I suggested it during his other visits?"

"Partly," her brother admitted. "But mostly it was because Brock isn't your home-cooked meal type. He's smooth and finished, like a diamond that's been cut into the perfect stone, hard and unfeeling."

"And diamonds don't sit down at a table set with ironstone flatware," Stephanie concluded in understanding.

"Something like that," Perry agreed. "Now, off with you," he ordered in a mock threat. "I have to find my notes for the luncheon speech."

She started for the door and hesitated short of her goal. "When will you be back—in case Brock asks?"

"Between half-past one and two."

"Maybe he'll be late," she suggested and walked to the door.

Forty-five minutes later, Perry stuck his head inside her office to let her know he was leaving to keep his luncheon engagement. "Take care of Brock if he arrives before I get back," he reminded her, unnecessarily.

"I will," she promised. "Good luck with the speech."

He waved and left. A few minutes later Stephanie closed her office to have lunch. Her appetite was all but nonexistent, so she chose a salad plate and picked at it for twenty minutes before giving up. A few minutes before one, she obtained the key to the private suite from Mary at the front desk and checked to be certain all was in readiness for Brock Canfield's arrival.

There had been no occasion for Stephanie to enter the private suite before. It consisted of a spacious sitting room, an equally large bedroom with a king-sized bed and an enormous bath. Stephanie explored it with unashamed curiosity.

Bronze-tipped, double-paned windows offered an unparalleled view of the White Mountains cloaked in their rust and gold autumn colors. Sunlight streaming through the glass laid a pattern of gold on the stark white floor of Italian ceramic, set in a herringbone design. There was nothing about the sitting room that resembled New England except for the scene outside its windows.

The furnishings included a white leather armchair and ottoman. A pair of short sofas were upholstered in natural Haitian cotton with coffee tables of antique white. The walls were covered with grass cloth in an ivory shade. A floor-to-ceiling cabinet, which included a shelf for a television to be rolled out, had been built into one wall. A glass-topped rattan table and four chairs were the only natural wood pieces in the room, besides an eight-foot-high secretary, hand carved in walnut. A gold-leaf, coromandel screen opened to reveal a bar. In total, it was an eclectic blend of periods and designs.

Stephanie took note of the bouquet of long-stemmed roses on the coffee table. The arrangement had an oriental touch with bare branches rising above the blood-red blooms. A vintage bottle of champagne was on ice in a silver bucket supported by a stud. A tray of cheese as well as an attractive bowl of fresh fruit was on the rattan table.

When Stephanie ventured into the bedroom, she stepped onto thick, shrimp-colored carpeting. The same color was repeated but dominated by black in the patterned bedspread and matching drapes. An ornate ebony headboard adorned the king-sized bed and was flanked by carved night-stands of the same dark hardwood. A hunting scene was depicted on an elephant tusk and a second was repeated in a massive collage. They gave the room the masculine accent.

The bathroom was a bit overwhelming in its luxury, with the shrimp carpeting extending into it. A white Jacuzzi bathtub was set in a platform faced with Italian marble that continued all the

way up to the ceiling. The wall area not covered
with marble was hung with black silk, a collection
of framed South American butterflies making use
of its backdrop. The bath towels were all a very
sensual black velour material, thick and rich looking.

Leaving the suite was like stepping into another
world. The inn was luxurious, but it attempted
to give its guests the flavor of New England. It
was obvious that Brock Canfield had decorated
the suite to please himself. Stephanie wasn't certain if she liked the result or whether she was
indulging in a little inverted snobbery.

As she entered the lobby, she thought she preferred the wide spaciousness of the white-painted
woodwork and its massive stone fireplace with
the welcoming warmth of the flames emitting the
pungent aroma of woodsmoke. Expensive Currier
and Ives lithographs adorned the white walls and
added the flavor of New England to the lobby.
The brass chandelier suspended from the ceiling
was a nuisance to clean, Stephanie knew, but the
hurricane globes were attractive and homey.

She stopped at the front desk to return the key.
"Any sign of Mr. Canfield yet, Mary?"

The mere mention of the owner's name seemed
to unnerve the usually calm woman. "Mr. Canfield? No, not that I know of. Ben, have you seen

him?'' She suddenly didn't trust her own answer and sought the confirmation of the bellboy.

"No. He hasn't arrived yet.'' He was much more positive.

"I'll be in my office," Stephanie replied. "Let me know as soon as he comes.''

Circling behind the registration counter, she walked down the short hallway to her office. She left the door open so she could be aware of the activity going on outside her four walls. The excited buzzing and whispering hadn't lessened since the news had circulated through the inn's grapevine of the imminent arrival of its owner. There was electricity in the air, and Stephanie wasn't immune to its volatile charge.

Before she put her bag away, she paused in front of the small mirror on a side wall to freshen her lipstick. But the new coat of bronzed pink on her mouth only accented the faint pallor in her cheeks. She stroked on a hint of blusher, then retouched her long lashes with mascara. By the time she was finished, she had completely redone her makeup.

Studying her reflection, she decided she was attractive but definitely not a raving beauty. The combination of thick chestnut hair and Corinthian-blue eyes was pleasing, but not startling. Her figure was slender with all the proper curves, but not eye-popping. There was a certain freshness about her, although she looked twenty-two.

All the while, she assured herself that this assessment had nothing to do with Brock Canfield or the warning Perry had given. Still, there was a little part of her that was wondering what it would be like if someone like Brock Canfield made a pass at her—a passing curiosity, no more than that, she insisted, just a flattering thought.

"Stephanie!" Mary hissed from the doorway. "*He* just drove up out front. Ben's going out to get his luggage now. And he has a woman with him."

Initially Stephanie smiled at the woman passing the information in such a frantic whisper. Who would hear? And what would it matter? But the last sentence wiped the smile from her face. Too late she remembered that in the past, Perry had mentioned that Brock Canfield often brought his current girl friend with him.

But what was the procedure? Did the woman stay in his suite? There wasn't any choice, was there? There wasn't a single other empty room in the entire inn. But she was attacked by the same uncertainty that Mary had suffered earlier, and the need to have someone back up her conclusion.

"Was Perry informed that Mr. Canfield was bringing a guest?" she asked the desk clerk.

"He didn't say anything to me about it," Mary replied with a negative shake of her head.

"Mr. Canfield wouldn't expect us to . . . have a separate room for her, would he?" There was no longer any need for the blusher on her cheeks. Mother Nature was doing an excellent job of providing color for Stephanie. "I mean, he didn't give us any warning."

"I seriously doubt if he wants her in a separate room." Mary's voice was both dry and suggestive. She glanced toward the lobby and quickly hissed, "He's coming through the door now!"

Stephanie took a deep breath to calm her suddenly jumping nerves and mentally crossed her fingers. Be calm, cool and collected, she told herself as she started toward the lobby. What did she have to be nervous about? Brock Canfield was only a man.

CHAPTER TWO

ONLY A MAN. That phrase Stephanie instantly revised the minute she saw the tall, dark-haired man in the lobby. Lean and virile, he was completely finished masculinity. The planes and contours of his tanned face had been chiseled into the final product of total manliness. An expensive topcoat hung from a set of broad shoulders and tapered slightly to indicate narrow hips before falling the length of his thighs to stop below the knees. Its dark color was contrasted by the white silk scarf around his neck.

Yet not for one minute did Stephanie believe that the elegant male attire covered a body that was other than superbly fit and muscled. It was evident in his ease of stride and natural coordination. Perry's description became very clear—

a hard, finished diamond. Brock Canfield was all that and all male.

Stephanie felt the awesome power of his attraction before she ever walked in front of the counter to greet him. It was even more potent when she came under the observation of his metallic gray eyes. Their lightness was compelling, at odds with the darkness of his brown hair.

His gaze made a thorough appraisal of her feminine assets as she crossed half the width of the lobby. His study was so openly one of male interest that she would have been offended if it had come from another man. But, no matter how hard she searched, she couldn't come up with any sense of indignation. Almost the exact opposite happened. Her pulse quickened with the inner excitement his look had generated.

Seeking a balance, she switched her attention to the blonde clinging to his arm. There was a surface impression of class and sophistication. Yet beneath it, Stephanie noticed the blue cashmere sweater was a size too small. The fine wool was stretched to emphasize the full roundness of the girl's breasts. So was the material in the complementing shade of darker blue pants that was forced to hug her hips and thighs.

Brock Canfield might regard the result as sexy and alluring, but Stephanie thought it was disgusting. Then she wondered if she was being bitchy. She didn't have time to decide as she reached the point where she had to speak.

"Hello, Mr. Canfield. I'm Stephanie Hall," she introduced herself, and offered her hand. "I hope you had a pleasant trip."

"An uneventful one." The grip of his hand was firm, its warmth seeming to spread up her arm and through her system. His gaze had narrowed in sharp curiosity. "Stephanie Hall," he repeated her name, his smooth voice giving it an unusual texture to the sound of her spoken name. "I wasn't aware Perry had got married. When did this happen?"

"Perry isn't married," she replied in quick surprise, then tried to explain. "At least not to me. I mean, he isn't married to anyone." She regained control of her wayward tongue and managed a more controlled, "I'm his sister."

"Ah, yes." He seemed to step back, to withdraw somehow, yet he didn't move except to release her hand. "I remember now that he mentioned he had a younger sister. Somehow I had the impression you were much younger."

Stephanie decided it was best if she didn't comment on that. "I'm sorry Perry isn't here to meet you himself, but he's a speaker at a club luncheon today. He should be back within the hour."

"Fine." His faint nod was indifferent. The blonde arched closer to him as if to remind him of her presence. It earned her a glance that was amused and tolerant, yet Stephanie detected no affection in his look. "Helen, I'd like you to meet Stephanie Hall, her brother manages the inn for me. This is Helen Collins."

But he deliberately omitted identifying the blonde's relationship to him. What could he have said? That she was his current mistress, his current lover? Stephanie wasn't certain if she could have handled such frankness. The glint in his eye made her suspect that Brock Canfield had guessed that. She didn't like the idea that he might find it—and her—amusing.

"May I show you to your suite?" Her stilted suggestion sounded as stiff and defensive as she felt.

"I think it would be an excellent idea." The line of his mouth was slanted in faint mockery.

The action pulled her gaze to his mouth. The firm set of male lips seemed to hint at worldly experience, their line strong and clean. Stephanie's curiosity ran rampant, wondering how expert they were.

Forcing a smile onto her mouth, she turned and walked to the desk to obtain the key from Mary. The woman slipped two keys into her outstretched palm. Out of the corner of her eye, Stephanie noticed Ben struggling with the luggage and knew he would be following them to the suite.

When she rejoined Brock Canfield and his female companion, the couple had already started in the general direction of the hall leading to the private suite. Stephanie would have preferred simply to give the man the keys, since he obviously knew the way, but she remembered Perry's instructions—take him to the suite and make sure he has everything he needs.

"Do you work here, Miss Hall? Or are you just helping your brother out?" The question came from Helen Collins, her tone on the acid side.

"I work here," she replied smoothly, and tried not to let her instinctive dislike of the blonde become obvious.

"In what capacity?" The masculine thickness of an eyebrow was arched in her direction, again assessing and appraising, but from an intellectual level.

"I take care of the books." Her answer was cool, prompted by an uncertainty whether Brock Canfield hadn't actually known or merely forgotten.

"So you're the reason the monthly reports have

suddenly become legible these last few months,''
he concluded.

Something in the remark had been faintly taunting. Stephanie was spared from replying as they
reached the suite. She unlocked the door and
quickly led the way inside, anxious to bring the
task to an end and regroup her scattered senses.

"It's stunning, Brock!" Helen exclaimed, be-
traying that it was her first visit to the suite. She
released his arm when she saw the roses on the
coffee table. "And roses! They're gorgeous. You
knew they were my favorite." She bent to inhale
the fragrance of one of the large blooms, and
Stephnie worried about the seam of her pants and
whether the thread could stand the strain.

"There's a bottle of champagne on ice for
you," Stephanie murmured and made a small
gesture with her hand in the general direction of
the silver bucket.

Brock Canfield's gray eyes skimmed her face,
their look mocking and amused, as if he sensed
her discomfort. There wasn't any need for him
to comment on the information, since Helen discovered the bottle of champagne seconds after-
ward.

"Darling, you think of everything," she declared, and plucked the bottle out of the ice. She

wrapped it in the towel and brought it to him. "Open it, Brock."

As he shrugged out of his topcoat, Stephanie saw her opening to be excused. "If there's anything else, Mr. Canfield—" she began.

"Don't leave yet, Miss Hall." His smooth order stopped the backward step Stephanie had taken to begin her retreat. But he offered no more explanation than the simple command that she remain.

She stood silently by, trying to appear as composed and calm as her jittery nerves would permit, while he tossed his coat and scarf over the white leather chair. A minute later his suit jacket joined them. Then he was expertly popping the cork out of the champagne bottle and filling the two glasses Helen had in her hands.

"Would you care to join us, Miss Hall?" he inquired. "There are more glasses in the bar."

"No, thank you," she refused with stiff politeness. "I have work to do this afternoon."

"One glass of champagne would interfere with your ability to function?" he mocked her, but returned the bottle to the ice bucket without reissuing his offer.

There was a knock at the door. Since Stephanie was closest, she answered it. It was Ben with the luggage. She motioned him inside the room.

"Put it in the bedroom," Helen instructed, and followed him to supervise.

"I think you'll find everything in order, Mr. Canfield." Stephanie tried again to make her exit. "I checked the suite myself before you arrived."

"I'm sure I will," he agreed.

Her opportunity was lost a second time as Ben came out of the bedroom. She was rather surprised when Brock gave him a tip for bringing the luggage. After all, he was the owner, so it wouldn't have been necessary. Ben thanked him and left.

"Here are your keys, Mr. Canfield." Stephanie crossed the front half of the room to give them to him.

He didn't immediately reach out to take them. Instead he turned to set the champagne glass on an antique white table. The white of his shirt complemented his supply muscled torso without emphasizing it. He looked lean and rangy like a wild animal on the prowl.

Minus the suit jacket, he appeared more casual, more approachable. Her unsteady pulse revealed the danger of such thinking, as she dropped the keys in his outstretched hand. The glitter of his gray eyes seemed to mock the action that avoided physical contact.

When Helen Collins appeared in the bedroom

doorway, his gaze slid from Stephanie. He didn't wait for the blonde to speak as he issued his instructions. "Unpack the suitcases, Helen, and make yourself comfortable. I'm going to be tied up for the afternoon."

He was politely but firmly telling his companion to get lost, dismissing her from his presence until he had time for the toy he had brought along to play with. Stephanie watched the curvaceous blonde smother the flash of resentment to smile and blow him a kiss before shutting the bedroom door.

"You don't approve of the arrangement, do you?" Amusement was threaded thickly through his question.

Stephanie worked to school her expression into one of indifference. "I wouldn't presume to pass judgment on your personal affairs, Mr. Canfield. They have nothing to do with me."

"Spoken with the true discretion of an employee to her indiscreet boss," he mocked her reply.

When he absently moved a step closer, Stephanie had to discipline her feet not to move back in an effort to keep a safe distance from him. Her nerve ends tingled with the sexual force of his attraction at such close quarters. The not unpleasant sensation triggered off a whole series of alarm bells in head.

"Will there be anything else, Mr. Canfield?" She made a show of glancing at her watch as if she was running late. "I really should be getting back to my office."

For a long second he held her gaze. Then his glance slid downward as he turned away and slipped the keys into his pocket. "You probably should." He picked up the glass of champagne.

Taking his agreement as permission to leave, Stephanie started toward the door. Relief was sweeping through her, the tension disintegrating with a rush. She could fully understand how curiosity killed the cat.

She was still five feet from the door when Brock Canfield stopped her with a low question. "Did your brother warn you about me?"

The plaid swirled around her knees as she pivoted to face him. "I beg your pardon?"

She felt cornered, trapped like a little brown mouse that almost escaped before a set of claws gently forced it back into the mouth of danger. A faintly wicked smile was deepening the corners of the firm male lips.

"Perry is very conscientious and thorough. That's why I made him manager," Brock stated and let his eyes run over her slender figure. "Surely he told you that I eat little girls like you for breakfast.'' He sipped at the champagne and gave Stephanie the impression he was drinking the essence of her.

Her throat worked convulsively for a second before she could get an answer out. ''Actually, I think Perry said you go through women like a gambler goes through decks of cards.'' She matched his frankness, but she was shaking inside.

''Very aptly put.'' His glass was lifted in a mock salute. ''Because generally I discard them after very little use—sometimes for no greater reason than that I want something new.'' Again, he took a drink of champagne and studied her with unnerving steadiness over the rim of the crystal glass. ''After all these years of keeping you hidden away, your brother took quite a risk sending you in his place. Why did he do it? Are you supposed to provide me with a distraction so I won't uncover some current problem?''

''There aren't any problems. Everything is running smoothly.'' She denied the suggestion that it was otherwise. ''Perry asked me to meet you because there wasn't anyone else. The night manager is at home sleeping and Perry's secretary is . . . terrified of you. That only left me to represent the managing staff, unless you throw out protocol. Then anyone would do.''

"She's a timid soul. Her name's Connie, isn't it?" Brock Canfield mused and wandered toward Stephanie. "Do you suppose she's afraid of sex?"

"She's naturally shy," Stephanie defended her brother's secretary, and fought the warmth that was trying to color her own cheeks.

When he reached her, Brock didn't stop but went on past her. She heard him set the glass on a table and started to turn. "Perry must have told you that if you become involved with me, I would hurt you."

His constant changing from directly personal to impersonal was keeping her off balance. Stephanie tried to adjust to this current reversal of tactics. He made a leisurely circle to stop on the opposite side of her. Her head turned slightly to bring him into the focus of her side vision. He didn't seem to expect a reply from her, and she didn't make one.

"It's true," he went on. "I know your kind. You eat Yankee pot roast on Sunday while I have Chateaubriand. I live out of hotel suites and you want a house with four bedrooms."

He reached out to lift the scarab pendant from her sweater and study it. His hand made no contact with her body, but the sensation was left, anyway. When he replaced it, his fingertips trailed down, tensing her stomach muscles.

"You want children, a boy and girl to mother, but I have no desire for an heir. It's time the Canfield name died." His gaze roamed to her breasts. The shallowness of her breathing had them barely moving beneath the ribbed knit of her sweater. "More than likely, you're the type that would want to nurse your babies yourself."

Stephanie didn't dispute any of his statements. She couldn't, because she guessed there was a fragment of truth in all of them. Her silence was ruled mostly by the knowledge that she was being seduced.

Brock Canfield was stating all the reasons why an affair with him would never last at the same time that he was persuading her to surrender to his desire, anyway. She couldn't raise a single objection when he was saying them all. It was crazy how helpless she felt.

When he moved to stand in front of her with only a hand's width separating their bodies, she was conscious of his maleness. Eye level with the lean breadth of his shoulders, she lifted her chin to study the strength of his masculine features, the darkness of his hair and the burnished silver of his eyes. He threaded his hands through the sides of her hair to frame her face.

"You want a man you can snuggle up to in bed and warm your cold feet," he said. "And

I want to enjoy a woman's body, then sleep alone on my side of the bed. We're oil and water. The combination doesn't mix.''

His gaze shifted to her lips. Her heartbeat faltered, then shifted into high gear, but she managed to control the downward drift of her eyelashes and kept them open, offering no silent invitation. Brock Canfield didn't need any. Her nerves tensed as his mouth descended toward hers with excruciating slowness.

First, the fanning warmth of his breath caressed her sensitive lips. Then she was assailed by the stimulating fragrance of some masculine cologne, the scent tinged with dry champagne. The hint of intoxication swirled through her senses an instant before his mouth moved expertly onto hers.

With persuasive ease, he sampled and tasted the soft curve of her lips, not attempting to eliminate the distance between them. Stephanie didn't relax nor resist the exploring kiss. Of their own accord, her lips clung to his for a split second as he casually ended the contact to brush his mouth against her cheek.

''You're a delectable morsel.'' His voice was deliberately pitched to a caressing level of huskiness. ''Maybe I'll save you for dessert.'' A light kiss tantalized the sensitive skin near her ear before he lifted his head to regard her with lazy gray eyes. "If you're smart, you'll slap my face, Stephanie."

"I'm smarter than that, Mr. Canfield." She was surprised she had a voice—and that it sounded so steady. "I'm not going to fight you—or in any way heighten your interest in the chase."

A smile of admiration spread across his face. It gentled the overwhelming virility of his tanned features. Stephanie's heart stopped beating for a full second, stunned by the potent charm the smile contained. He untangled his hands from her hair and stepped away to reclaim his champagne glass.

"Now you've intrigued me, Stephanie," he murmured, and downed the swallow of champagne.

"Believe me, that wasn't my intention." Agitation stirred her voice.

"Wasn't it?" Brock challenged with a knowing lift of a dark eyebrow.

"No." But she couldn't hold his gaze so she looked away, lifting her chin a fraction of an inch higher.

The phone rang and Brock walked away from it, ordering over his shoulder, "Answer it."

Stephanie hesitated, then stepped to pick up the white receiver. "Yes? Mr. Canfield's suite."

"Stephanie?" It was her brother calling. He

sounded surprised that she had answered. "Connie said Brock arrived fifteen minutes ago. Why are you still there? Any problems?"

"No, I was just leaving." She was glad her voice sounded normal and not as emotionally charged as she felt. "Mr. Canfield is right here. Would you like to speak to him?"

"Yes, put him on," Perry agreed to her suggestion a little thoughtfully.

She held out the receiver to Brock. "It's Perry."

He walked over to take the phone from her hand, without attempting to touch her. His hand covered the mouthpiece. "It's a pity we have to postpone our discussion just when it was becoming interesting."

She refused to rise to his bait. "I hope you enjoy your stay with us," she offered, as if she was addressing a hotel guest instead of the owner.

As she turned to walk to the door, his voice followed her. "That remains to be seen, Stephanie."

His remark held the hint of a promise that their discussion would be resumed at a later time. The part of her that wasn't ruled by common sense was looking forward to it.

Crossing the threshold into the hallway, Stephanie half turned to close the door. Her gaze was drawn to the leanly muscled man on the phone, but he had already forgotten her. His dark head bent in concentration as he listened to what Perry was saying. Very quietly she shut the door and walked swiftly down the carpeted hallway.

When she reached her office, she closed its door. It was a defense mechanism to prevent her from watching for Brock Canfield. She paused long enough at the mirror to smooth the hair his hands had rumpled, then spread the daily entry sheet on her desk and started to work.

Once she heard Perry and Brock's voice in the hall outside her office. Unconsciously she held her breath, but they didn't stop. She guessed her brother was taking Brock on a brief tour of the inner workings of the inn. It sounded logical although Brock was probably very familiar with all that went on.

Late in the afternoon, Perry knocked on her door and walked in. "Stephanie, do you have those cost projections on renovating the pool house into a sauna and exercise club?"

Her gaze ricocheted off her brother to be stopped by the masked gleam of Brock's gray eyes. A charcoal pullover had taken the place of his tie, the white collar of his shirt extending over the neckline of the sweater. The casual attire didn't diminish the air of male authority that draped him like a second skin.

"I have a copy." She dragged her gaze from Brock to open a side desk drawer. "I believe I saw yours at home."

"That's right," Perry remembered. "It's in the library on the desk." He took the portfolio Stephanie handed him and passed it to Brock. "As you can see on page two, the cost of equipping it is within range of the estimate. The main stumbling block is this bearing wall." He unrolled the architect's drawing on Stephanie's desk to show Brock where the difficulty had arisen in revamping the pool house.

Stephanie leaned back in her chair, unable to work while the two men discussed the problem. The inaction gave her too much freedom to study Brock Canfield. Sitting sideways on the edge of her desk, he listened attentively to Perry's explanations and counterproposals.

His position pulled the material of his slacks tautly over his thigh as his muscles bunched beneath it. She liked the clean, strong lines of his profile, the vibrant thickness of his dark brown hair and his lean, well-muscled build.

What bothered her was his innate sex appeal that didn't rely on good looks. He was handsome in a hard kind of way, but it was much more than that. She couldn't look at him without being aware that he was a man.

All the warnings didn't mean a damn, Stephanie realized—not coming from Perry or Brock. It was like being warned against the dangers of getting too close to a fire when she was shivering. She'd take the risk for the chance to be warmed by the flames. Glancing away from the compelling figure half-seated on her desk, she nervously moistened her lips as she realized what she was admitting.

When she looked back at Brock, he was watching her, a smile in the gray depths of his eyes as if he knew what she was thinking and the decision she had reached. It was totally impossible. But she didn't draw an easy breath until he returned his attention to the green portfolio.

"Let me make a suggestion, Perry," he said. "I'll study these blueprints and the cost projections and we'll discuss it this evening. You and your sister can join me for dinner." He straightened from her desk, his glance barely touching her as he bent to roll the blueprints. "Have you made other plans for dinner?" The question was an afterthought, addressed to her brother, not Stephanie.

"I'm free this evening, but I can't speak for Stephanie." There was a silent warning in the look Perry gave her, that said he would back up any excuse she chose to give.

"You'll come to keep the numbers even, won't you?" The statement was issued in the guise of a question as Brock studied her with knowing certainty. "You and Helen can gossip while Perry and I discuss business."

"We could always postpone it until morning," Perry suggested.

"Business before pleasure," Brock insisted with a glance in the general direction of her brother before his gaze returned to lock with hers. "Shall we meet at eight o'clock in the restaurant? That will give you time to go home and change."

"Eight o'clock will be fine," Stephanie agreed as she had known she would all along.

Perry gave her a look that said she had taken leave of her senses—but that was precisely what had happened. It didn't matter how foolish or futile it seemed. She was way out of her league with Brock Canfield, and there was no future in pursuing a relationship with him.

But she wasn't ruled by logic. A more powerful force was directing her actions.

CHAPTER THREE

"DID HE make a pass at you?" Perry slipped the curly jacket over her shoulders, his hands lingering for a second.

"Of course." At his muffled curse Stephanie laughed. "That shouldn't come as a surprise to you. You did warn me that he would."

The laughter eased the tension gnawing at her nerve ends. Dining out was a luxury that they had rarely been able to afford. It was rarer still when her occasional dates had taken her out to dinner. Therefore her wardrobe was sadly lacking in dressy clothes.

The simple lines of the rust-colored dress came the closest to being what Stephanie deemed appropriate to wear. To it she added a plain gold belt and two strands of gold chain to overlap the jewel neckline. She tried to consider her choice as understated elegance as opposed to under-dressed.

Luckily, Perry hadn't arrived at the house until twenty minutes ago, so he didn't know how she had agonized over what to wear. He had barely had time to shower and change into a fresh suit and tie. His brown hair still glistened from the shower spray. She could feel him eyeing her with brotherly concern while she buttoned the short jacket.

"What happened, Stephanie?" he questioned with less anger.

Turning to face him, she made a pretense of straightening his tie. "I didn't swoon at his feet, if that's what's worrying you," she joked.

"Will you be serious?" Perry insisted, acting every inch the wise older brother. "I can assure you that Brock isn't regarding it so lightly."

"Probably not," Stephanie conceded, sobering a little.

"Listen, if you want to change your mind, I'll make an excuse for you. One of your friends drove up for the weekend or something," he suggested.

"And fix something to eat when I can dine out? No, thanks." She shook her head in definite refusal. "Besides, you're going to be there to chaperon me. Not to mention the fact that his girl friend will be with us, too.'' The thought left a bad taste in her mouth. She moved to the front door. ''We only have ten minutes to make it to the inn.''

''I forgot about the girl he brought along.'' Perry followed her out of the house to the station wagon that belonged to the inn. There was a frown in his expression when he opened the car door for her. ''Are you attracted to him, Stephanie?''

''I wouldn't be normal if I wasn't,'' she admitted. ''Don't look so worried, Perry. It's better that I know it and admit it than have it hit me all of a sudden one day when it's too late.''

''I suppose there's some logic in that thinking.'' But he didn't sound convinced.

When her door was shut, he walked around the front of the car to slide in the driver's side. Stephanie studied his grim profile as he started the motor. Impulsively, she reached out to touch his arm.

''Try not to worry about me too much, Perry,'' she said. ''I know you'd like to fight all my battles, big brother, but some of them I have to face alone.''

''I'm being overprotective,'' he admitted. ''But

it's become a habit to look after you. It's hard to remember that you're an adult.''

"I know." And Stephanie did understand. She didn't resent the concern Perry voiced, because she knew his intentions were the best.

Tactfully, he switched the subject to the renovations of the pool house, which had been his idea. He was certain it would enhance the overall appeal of the inn and ensure their ability to compete with the newer, more modern ski lodges in the area. So far, Brock hadn't vetoed the plan, which made tonight very important.

The inn possessed two restaurants, but the formal dining room was only open during the evening dinner hour. It was one of the few dining rooms in the area that required proper attire, yet it was rarely empty. After spending the day hiking, skiing or cycling, guests seemed to welcome the excuse to dress up. Local residents often dined there as well, making reservations almost a necessity. This Friday was no exception.

After leaving her jacket at the coat check, Stephanie let Perry escort her to the table where Brock and his blond companion were waiting. Brock rose at their approach, his dark elegance reaching out to ensnare Stephanie. A ghost of a smile touched his mouth as he met her look. She felt oddly breathless, but her reflection in the mirrored wall didn't show this inner disturbance.

"Have you been waiting long?" Perry asked, more out of politeness than concern that they were late.

"No, Helen and I have just arrived. I don't believe you've met Helen Collins," Brock introduced. "My manager, Perry Hall. Of course, you member his sister Stephanie."

Stephanie received no more than a cursory glance from the blonde, who did manage to smile at Perry. It was obvious by the forced pleasure in her expression that Helen resented their presence. She had probably looked forward to having Brock all to herself that evening, Stephanie realized.

That little trill of gladness that sang in her veins was the result of suppressed jealousy. The discovery brought Stephanie briefly to her senses. She wasn't going to spend the entire evening being envious of the slightest attention Brock paid to Helen.

"Sit here, Perry." Brock indicated the empty chair to his left. "That way we'll be able to talk without having to shout across the table."

Which left the chair opposite him for Stephanie. She wouldn't be sitting beside him, but she would be facing him through dinner. She knew she would have to guard against staring at him. Something told her Helen Collins wouldn't be very talkative.

It proved to be a very accurate prediction. Courtesy insisted that Stephanie make some initial attempts to start a conversation by inquiring where Helen was from, etcetera. When the other girl made no attempt to keep the conversation going, Stephanie didn't, either.

In consequence, she sat through dinner listening to the two men discuss the proposed renovations. She didn't find it boring. On the contrary, she was fascinated by the quickness of Brock's mind—shrewd and astute. And she was rather proud of Perry's ability to keep up with his fast-thinking employer.

But it became increasingly obvious that Helen didn't share Stephanie's appreciation of the conversation. She began smoking incessantly, since it gave her an excuse to interrupt the talk to have Brock light her cigarette. Stephanie was more embarrassed than envious of the way Helen gazed so limpidly into Brock's eyes and bent closer as if inviting his embrace. Brock's reaction was a mixture of aloofness, tolerance and amusement.

Occasionally his glance did stray to Stephanie, but he made no attempt to flirt with her. She was glad, because it would have made a mockery of the business discussion with her brother if he had.

After the dinner plates were removed, the waiter wheeled the dessert cart to the table. "Aren't you going to have something, Brock?" Helen protested when everyone ordered something except him.

"No." He gave her a lazy smile that remained in his expression when he glanced around the table. "I'll have my dessert later." His gaze lingered for a fraction of a second on Stephanie.

Her recall was instant and vivid, remembering that he had mentioned saving her for dessert. There was a wild fluttering in her stomach as she quickly dropped her gaze to the bowl of sweetened fresh fruit in front of her.

She was constantly off-balance with him. Just when she had become used to being ignored, he had reminded her of that intimate remark. Somehow she had to learn to keep both feet solidly on the ground whenever she was around him. It was the only way she would survive this tumultuous interlude.

"The dining room closes at ten, Mr. Canfield," Stephanie remarked. "If you want dessert, perhaps you should have it now."

"Now?" His mouth twitched with a smile as his gaze dared her to repeat that challenge. "I'd rather have it later. If it happens to be after ten, and the craving is too great, I'll simply raid the refrigerator.''

''If you'd like, I can arrange to have a selection sent up to your suite,'' Perry suggested, and Stephanie nearly choked on a strawberry.

''Can you?'' There was a wealth of understated meaning to Brock's droll response. ''I'll try to remember that.'' The waiter was at his elbow with the silver coffee pot. ''Yes, black, please.''

While they finished their coffee and dessert, it was decided that Perry would contact the architect and arrange a meeting early on Saturday morning. Brock had changes he wanted made in the plans before he gave his final approval. Stephanie knew her brother's sense of achievement at Brock's acceptance of his idea and felt proud for him.

''I'm beginning to get the feeling your talents are not being fully utilized at the inn,'' Brock remarked, studying Perry with a narrowed look. ''Is this your ambition? To be in charge of a place like this?''

Perry hesitated, darting Stephanie a quick look. His uncertainty was obvious. ''I wouldn't say it's my sole ambition, but I find it challenging, always different.''

"That's a diplomatic answer. Now, what's the truth?" Brock challenged.

"That's the truth," Perry laughed, but insincerely.

"The truth is, Mr. Canfield, that Perry has always wanted to be a lawyer," Stephanie inserted, disregarding the silencing look her brother sent.

"What stopped you? I've seen your college transcripts."

"My father had a skiing accident. I was needed at home," her brother explained simply and immediately changed the subject. "The long-range forecast for the winter calls for a lot of snow. It's predicted the area will have its best ski season to date."

"The reservations show it." Stephanie followed his lead, her way of apologizing for bringing up the education he had been forced to abandon. "We're booked solid all the way to March."

"I noticed." Brock went along with the new topic.

"Excuse me." The brittle words were issued by Helen as she pushed away from the table to stand. "I'm going to the powder room to freshen my lipstick."

Brock caught at her hand. "We'll meet you in the lounge. Don't be long."

The sullen look was immediately replaced by a bright smile. "I won't," the blonde promised and hurried away with a provocative sway of her hips.

"We should be going home," Stephanie murmured to her brother.

"Yes, it is late," he agreed, with a glance at his watch.

"Have one drink with us," Brock insisted. "We haven't toasted your new plan. It was a brilliant idea of yours, Perry, to utilize an existing building for the sauna, especially since it's virtually unused. It makes an already attractive package both practical and economical."

"I'm glad you think so, Brock," her brother replied modestly. "But I'm certain you would have come up with the plan if I'd suggested building an entirely new building."

"I hope so." Again there was that wide smile, all lazy charm. "How about that drink? Will you join us?"

After exchanging a glance with Stephanie, Perry agreed. "Just one. We don't want to intrude any further on your evening."

"Just one," Brock nodded.

He was at her chair when Stephanie rose. His hand seemed to find its way to her waist to guide her to the side door leading to the lounge. His touch was lightly possessive, impersonal yet warm. She could feel the imprint of his fingers through the material of her dress. The sensation seemed to brand her as his property.

The lounge was crowded, as it generally was on the weekends. A dance combo was playing, sprayed by a rotating rainbow of lights in the otherwise dark room. During the off-season, the inn only had live entertainment on the weekends. In the winter, when the White Mountains were filled with skiers, they had a group seven nights a week.

Brock found an empty booth in a far corner of the room. By the time they had ordered a round of drinks, Helen arrived. She ignored his invitation to join them and instead coaxed Brock onto the dance floor. Stephanie watched the blonde become the sultry enchantress, weaving her web around Brock, and knew she could never compete with such tactics.

"Would you like to dance?" Perry suggested.

Stephanie glanced up to refuse, but one look at the challenging gleam in his eyes made her realize how dispirited she had become in the span of a few minutes. A faintly chagrined smile curved her mouth as she nodded acceptance of his invitation.

Once on the dance floor, the swinging music

soon made its upbeat rhythm felt. Concentrating on the dance steps distracted her from the sight of Helen with Brock. Also there was the knowledge that she and Perry danced well together, their steps always matching, but he had also been the one who taught her how.

When the song ended, she was breathless and laughing. "Feel better?" Perry smiled as he guided her off the dance floor.

"Much better," she agreed, glancing over her shoulders to smile at him. "Thanks."

The lights were dimmed to a single blue color for a slow number. Her eyes didn't adjust immediately to the change of light, and she had to stop for a minute to keep from running into a table or chair in the semidarkness.

Her gaze saw Brock and Helen on a course parallel with theirs. He bent his head to murmur something to the blonde, who didn't look pleased by his statement. Then he was leaving Helen to make her way back to the booth alone, and crossing to intercept Stephanie.

"You don't object if I have this dance with your sister before you leave, do you, Perry?" Brock asked, although Stephanie didn't know why. He had already taken hold of her arm to direct her back to the dance floor.

She was certain Perry answered him, but she

didn't hear what was said. Almost the instant they reached the cleared area, Brock was turning her into his arms. As usual, there were more couples on the floor to dance to the slow tunes, so it became less a matter of dancing and more a matter of avoiding others. They were soon swallowed into the center of the group.

He folded her arm against his chest while his hand slid up her spine to force her closer. Stephanie could feel her heart thudding against her ribs as they swayed together, moving their feet without going anywhere. Ultimately she became conscious of the hard wall of his chest, the flatness of his stomach and the leg shifting between hers in rhythm with the music.

When he released her hand to leave it against the lapel of his jacket, Brock seemed to give up all pretense of dancing. Both arms were around her, his fingers spread as they roamed over her shoulders, ribs and spine, slowly caressing and molding her to him.

Stephanie could barely breathe. This was what she had wanted all evening, yet she couldn't relax. She felt like a child who had been given a giant lollipop and was afraid to enjoy it too much, because she knew it was going to be taken away from her.

His chin rubbed against her temple, his breath

stirring her hair. A silent whimper of suppressed delight sighed through her when he turned his mouth against her, investigating the corner of her eye and the curve of her cheekbone.

"I could develop a sweet tooth for dessert." Finding her ear, he nuzzled aside the silken chestnut hair covering it to let his moist lips nibble at the lobe, shattering her equilibrium.

In another second she was going to melt like a piece of sugar on his tongue. "You already have." Her voice wasn't all that strong, the words coming out in a thin, taut whisper.

"Is that right?" His mouth curved against the skin of her cheek.

All she had to do was lift her head and Brock would find her lips, but she lowered her chin a fraction of an inch. Her eyes were closed by the feathery brush of his mouth across her lashes.

"Any member of the opposite sex would satisfy you when you're in an amorous mood," she insisted, because she knew it was true. Brock was pursuing her because she was new, not because he thought she was special. It was a fact she acknowledged without bitterness. "You have such a healthy appetite that you bring your nighttime treats along with you."

"But you're the one in my arms. Why don't you satisfy me?" he challenged softly.

Her heart ran away with itself at the thought of satisfying him and being satisfied by him. His virility was a potent force that left her weak. She could imagine the devastation his practiced skill could wreak if she let herself become carried away by it. Someone jostled her shoulder in the melee of dancing couples and her head lifted in faint surprise.

In the next second, she was immobilized by the touch of his mouth against the corner of her lips. Then she was turning to seek the completeness of it, mindless of the others around them. It was a devouring kiss, hard and demanding, ending within seconds after it had begun. It hadn't seemed to help that she had both feet on the floor. Discretion had been swept aside so easily.

"Do you do this with all your women? Make love to them on the dance floor? First Helen, now me." She found the strength to mock him, although her voice was a little shaky.

Her head was still tipped back, enabling her to look into his eyes. The dim interior of the lounge had enlarged the black pupils, leaving a thin silver ring around them. They were smiling at her, with an inner satisfaction and supreme confidence, certain of his ability to seduce her.

Stephanie supposed she was transparent. Her pride was injured that she was such an easy conquest for him. But was there a woman born who could deny his attraction for long?

"I've aroused you, despite that cool and composed expression you're wearing," Brock stated. Cool? Composed? Her? It seemed impossible. His hand moved to caress her neck, stopping when it found her pulse point. She could feel it and hear it hammering against his fingertip. "Your pulse is racing. Feel what you're doing to me."

Taking her fingers, he carried them to his neck and pressed them to the throbbing vein. She felt its wild beat, not so far behind the swift tempo of her own. Had she disturbed him? Or was it only desire? She had felt safer with the jacket beneath her fingers rather than the vital warmth of his skin.

"Your hand feels cool," he murmured.

That seemed impossible when she felt hot all over. When she tried to withdraw her fingers from his grasp, it tightened. He lifted her hand to his mouth and sensually kissed the center of her palm.

"I want you, Stephanie," he said as the last note of the song faded and the rainbow of lights came on.

The sudden murmur of voices shattered the intimacy of the moment. Stephanie didn't have to find an answer to that heady comment as the exiting dancers forced them apart. He retained his hold of her hand while she let the crowd lead her off the floor.

Fixing her gaze on Perry in the far booth, she weaved her way through the tables. Before she reached it, she gave a little tug to free her hand from Brock's grip. He let it go without protest. She didn't squarely meet the look her brother gave her when she slid onto the booth seat beside him. Her glance darted across the table to Helen, whose bored and impatient expression spoke volumes.

"I hope you've finally fulfilled all your obligations for the evening, Brock," Helen voiced her irritation at being left to her own devices for so much of the evening.

"Stop bitching, Helen." As he sat down, he stretched his arm across the backrest behind the blonde and picked up his drink. "I warned you this would be a business trip." It was a lazy reminder, a steel edge cloaked in velvet tones.

Over the rim of his glass, his gaze locked with Stephanie's. She read his message of dissatisfaction and desire, schooled with patience. She took a sip of her own drink, but the ice had melted, diluting it and leaving it flat and tasteless. She set it down and pushed it aside to glance at her brother.

"It's getting late, Perry. We should be going." Knowing he would agree, she rose and moved aside so he could slide out.

"I'll see you in the morning, Brock." He shook hands with Brock, who was also standing.

"It was a pleasure meeting you, Miss Collins." Stephanie nodded at the blonde, not caring that it was only a polite phrase she offered. Her only response was an indifferent glance. Then she addressed Brock. "You're leaving on Sunday, aren't you?"

"Yes, late in the afternoon," he acknowledged with a slight narrowing of his gaze.

"I doubt if I'll see you again before you leave, so I hope you have a safe trip." She placed her hand in his.

Brock held on to it when she would have withdrawn it. "Aren't you working tomorrow?"

"No." Conscious of Perry at her side, she sent him a sideways glance, smiling. "I have a great boss. He gives me the weekends off so I can do his laundry and clean the house."

He released her hand somewhat absently and smiled at her brother. "Good night. I'll meet you in the morning around eight."

Before they had taken a step away from the booth, Brock was sitting down and turning his attention to Helen, who was suddenly all smiles.

Stephanie tried desperately not to remember that only moments before he had been holding her in his arms. Now someone else was going to satisfy him. She didn't do a very good job of convincing herself that she was the lucky one to be walking away relatively unscathed.

They stopped at the coat check for Stephanie's jacket and Perry's overcoat. Both were silent as they walked outside into the crisp autumn night to the station wagon.

The only thing that was said during the drive home came when Perry remarked, ''I hope you know what you're doing, Stephanie.''

''So do I,'' she sighed.

CHAPTER FOUR

THE DIRTY breakfast dishes were stacked in the sink. Stephanie paused at the counter to drink the last swallow of coffee from her cup. Her gaze automatically wandered out of the window above the sink to the foothills emblazoned with the reds and golds of autumn.

In the back of the old farmhouse, a brook rushed through the rolling acreage, complete with a romantic stone bridge crossing it. Cords of firewood were stacked near the back door of the house—fuel for the cold New England winter.

Sighing, she turned away from the beauty of the clear autumn morning and set her cup with the rest of the dishes. She'd wash them later. Right now she wanted the hot water for the first load of clothes.

The back porch doubled as the washroom; a washer and dryer were ensconced in one corner. The small floor space was littered with baskets and piles of dirty clothes that Stephanie set about separating into individual loads, tossing the white clothes directly into the washing machine.

It was a nice enough day that she could hang the clothes on the line to dry. Besides, the clothes always smelled so much cleaner and fresher that way.

She pushed the sleeves of the old gray sweat shirt up to her elbows. It was one of Perry's, which meant it was several sizes too large for her, but it was comfortable to work in and it didn't matter if she spilled bleach on it. Her blue jeans were faded and shrunk from numerous washings and snugly hugged her slender hips and thighs, but the denim material was soft like a second skin.

Her hair was pulled away from her face into a ridiculously short ponytail, secured with a piece of blue yarn. She hadn't bothered with makeup. By the time she washed the clothes, dusted the furniture and swept the floors of the two-story farmhouse, there wouldn't be any trace of it left, anyway. Besides, the only one who came on Saturday mornings was Mrs. Hammermill with fresh eggs for the week.

When there was a knock at the front door, Stephanie didn't hesitate over who it might be. "Come in!" she shouted, and continued separating the clothes. At the sound of the door opening, then closing, she added, "I'm in the kitchen, Mrs. Hammermill," which was close enough to her location. "You can put the eggs on the counter. If you have an extra dozen, I'll take them. Perry mentioned he'd like an angel food cake. I thought I'd try my hand at making one from scratch this afternoon."

There was a movement in the doorway to the porch, but Stephanie didn't glance up. She was busy examining the white shirt in her hand that Perry had somehow managed to mark up the front of with ball-point ink.

"You don't happen to know what I can use to get this ink out of Perry's shirt, do you?" she frowned. "I've tried just about everything at one time or another and . . . . When she looked up, she saw Brock leaning a shoulder against the doorjamb, his arms crossed. She froze at the sight of him. "Brock!" His name was startled from her.

"Try hairspray. My secretary swears by it," he suggested with a trace of teasing amusement in his droll voice. His corduroy pants were desert brown, the same shade as the heavy sweater with the stag's head design on the chest.

Her gaze flew past him to the cat clock on the kitchen wall with its switching tail for a pendulum. It was a few minutes before half-past eight.

"What are you doing here?" she asked in confusion, still clutching the shirt and standing amid the piles of dirty clothes. "I thought you were—"

"The egg lady? Yes, I know." He finished the sentence for her and uncrossed his arms to stand up straight. "The answer to your question should be obvious. I came to see you."

"Yes, but . . . you were supposed to meet Perry this morning," Stephanie said in vague protest.

"I did . . . for a few minutes. Are you going to come here? Or am I going to have to wade through all those clothes to get to you?" He both challenged and mocked her.

Stephanie laid the shirt over the side of the washing machine. In doing so, she became conscious of her appearance. Her gaze slid down the front of her sloppy sweat shirt and faded jeans. She felt the nakedness of her face, minus even lipstick.

"You should have called before coming over." Raising a hand to the hair tied back, she stepped over the pile of clothes blocking her path to the doorway and Brock.

"If I had, I wouldn't have got the chance to see this domestic scene." Brock reached out to take the hand she was balancing with and pulled her into his arms, locking his hands behind her back while he studied her upturned face. "And you know you look like a sexy little girl in that outfit."

It wasn't exactly the compliment she wanted to hear as she turned her head away to let his kiss land on her cheek and pushed her way past him into the kitchen. The floor seemed to roll under her feet, but she knew it was only her knees quaking.

"I don't want to look like a little girl," she declared, and lifted both her hands to untie the knotted yarn around her hair. But she had tied it tight and the knot defied the attempts of her trembling fingers to loosen it.

When she felt Brock's push hers out of the way, she tried to move away, but he clamped a hand on her shoulder to keep her in place. "Hold still," he ordered, and Stephanie stood quietly while he worked the yarn free of the knot. When it was untied, he turned her around and combed her hair into place with his fingers. "Now you just look sexy. Are you happy?" he asked with a lazy glint in his gray eyes.

But he didn't wait for her to answer, he bent

his head to cover her lips with his mouth, skillfully parting them as he curved her into his arms. Her fingers curled into the wool of his sweater, clinging to the only solid thing she could find in the deepening intensity of his kiss. She was exposed to a whole set of raw, new emotions that had her straining toward him in trembling need. He dragged his mouth roughly across her cheek to her ear.

"Did you really think you wouldn't see me again before I left?" He sounded almost angry.

"I'm not sure if I believed it or not," Stephanie admitted with her eyes closed as he nibbled his way down her neck to her shoulder.

"Where are your parents? Who else are you expecting besides the egg lady?" he demanded.

"My parents are dead," she whispered, and wondered why he didn't know that. "There's only Mrs. Hammermill. She usually comes before nine."

She felt as well as heard the deep shuddering breath Brock took before he lifted his head to smile tightly at her. "In that case, why don't you fix me some breakfast? I didn't bother to eat before I came over. I thought you might do your shopping in the morning and I didn't want to miss you."

Not knowing how much she dared into that

statement, Stephanie decided not to comment on it. "Do you want bacon and eggs?" she asked instead.

"What I want, I can't have at the moment." His hands slid up her back, suggestively pressing her closer to him before he released her and stepped away. "Bacon and eggs will do."

"How do you like your eggs?" She walked to the refrigerator, glad to have something to do. She took out the package of bacon and the last two eggs from the shelf.

"Sunny-side up, and crisp bacon."

She spied the pitcher of orange juice on the refrigerator shelf. "Juice?"

"No, thanks." Brock came to stand beside her while she laid the bacon strips in the skillet.

When it began to sizzle, she walked to the cupboard on the other side of him and took down a place setting. She glanced uncertainly at the kitchen table, then at him. "Would you like to eat in the dining room?" she suggested.

"No," he said with a decisive shake of his head. "I have no intention of letting you out of my sight."

His look, as well as his answer, was disturbing, but it also gave her such much-needed confidence. She was smiling as she arranged the plate and cutlery on the gingham-clothed kitchen table. She walked back to the stove to turn the bacon.

"When was the last time you had breakfast in somebody's kitchen?" she asked curiously, eyeing him with a sidelong glance.

"Probably not since I was a child," he admitted what Stephanie had suspected. "Are you a good cook?"

"Not as good as Perry, but he's had a lot more practice than I have." The bacon was beginning to brown nicely, so Stephanie kept turning it.

Brock took up a position behind her, his hands caressing the curve of her shoulders, while his thumbs rubbed the hollows of her neck. "Why did he have more practice?" He didn't really sound interested in the subject.

"Our mother died when I was only four. Since our father had to work at two jobs to support us, Perry had to do the cooking and look after me."

It was difficult to concentrate on what she was doing under the caress of his hands. She managed to rescue the bacon before it was burned and set it aside to drain on a paper towel.

"What did your father do?"

"He considered himself a ski instructor, but mostly he earned money as a bartender and cutting firewood . . . until his accident." She cracked the eggs and slipped them into the hot bacon fat.

"The accident that forced your brother to give up his law career," Brock guessed.

"Yes, he was crippled in a skiing accident." She looked over her shoulder, a curious frown knitting her forehead. "Perry has worked for you for over five years. Surely you knew that."

"No. I don't bother to inquire about the personal lives of my employees unless it affects their work. There's never been any reason to fault your brother's work." There was an indifferent and dismissing shrug of his shoulders.

"But surely you want to know something about their backgrounds," Stephanie insisted.

"Only their qualifications for their particular position. As long as I get the results I want, I couldn't care less who or what they are as individuals." There was a curve to his mouth, but it wasn't a smile. "You think that's a very callous attitude, don't you?"

She concentrated her gaze on the eggs in the skillet, the bright yellow yolks staring back at her. "Yes, I do."

"White Boar Inn represents half of one percent of the gross business Canfield Enterprises earns annually. Maybe that will give you an idea of how many Perry Halls I have working for me," he suggested. "I couldn't possibly become involved or have knowledge of their personal lives without losing perspective of my overall responsibility. By rights, I should sell the inn.''

"Why don't you?'' She could see the logic in his argument, but she mentally recoiled from this evidence of his lack of feeling. The eggs were done, so she moved away to fetch his plate from the table and scoop them onto it with the spatula.

"For personal reasons,'' Brock answered. Stephanie didn't think he intended to explain what they were, but she was wrong. "My parents spent their honeymoon at the White Boar when they eloped. He bought it for her on their sixth anniversary. He was the one who decreed that the honeymoon suite would be reserved only for Canfields.''

"No wonder you're reluctant to sell it.'' Her smile was soft and radiant when she gazed at him, touched by this unexpected display of sentiment.

"Six months after he bought it, they went through a messy divorce that lasted two years. My mother has since remarried several times. My father, wisely, contented himself with a stream of mistresses.'' Brock watched her smile fade almost with satisfaction.

"Is . . . is he living?'' Averting her gaze, Stephanie walked past him, carrying the plate of eggs and bacon to the table.

"Yes. He's retired to the south of France. I believe his current lover is a twenty-year-old model." Brock followed her. "Of course, he refers to her as his protégée."

"Coffee?" When she set his plate down, she searched for an excuse to find something else to do.

"Black with no sugar."

Stephanie moved away from the table as he sat down to eat. "You must not have had a very happy childhood," she guessed.

"That depends on your definition of happy. My grandfather raised me even before my parents were divorced. They were always vacationing in some exotic resort in a far-off corner of the world. The divorce had little effect on me. Most of the time I was away at school or else with my grandfather. From the day I was born I was groomed to take over the company, and when my grandfather died a few years ago, that's exactly what I did."

Stephanie poured two cups and carried them to the table. "And the last time you ate in somebody's kitchen, that was with your grandfather?"

"Hardly." Brock laughed shortly. "He had all his meals at his desk unless it was a business dinner. No, I spent a week at the home of one of my classmates."

"Why don't you sell the inn?" Stephanie watched him, half-afraid to hear his answer. "It's obvious that you feel no sentimental attachment to it."

Brock was slow to answer, but it wasn't due to any hesitancy. "It reminds me that intimate relationships don't necessarily last forever no matter how strong the attachment appears on the surface."

"You make the trip here on an average of four times a year. Yet I've never heard of you bringing the same woman twice. Is that why?" But that question simply prompted another. "Why did you come this morning when Helen is back in the suite?"

"Because I didn't want to be with her. I wanted to be with you." His sharpness dissolved into a chuckle. "You are having a hard time trying to understand me, aren't you? The Helens of this world go in and out of my life all the time. I have the sex drive of any normal male. There's no pretense, on either side, that we're together for any reason other than the purely physical—or sexual—if you prefer. She understood the ground rules going in—no emotional claims on me or my time. In return, I treat her with respect and courtesy. I'm not attempting to brag or shock you: I'm only trying to explain the circumstances that dictate my life-style."

Stephanie was trying but it all sounded very cold-blooded. "I am sure you can rationalize any behavior," she replied stiffly.

Leaning forward in his chair, Brock reached for her hand and gripped it firmly in his. The intensity of his gaze was piercing. "What I'm not making clear to you, Stephanie, is how difficult it is for me to have the kind of relationship you regard as normal—with any woman. I don't have time to carry out a courtship." A muscle was working convulsively along his jaw. "Tomorrow I'm driving to New York. When I arrive, there might be a phone call that will take me to the West Coast. I could be there a month, maybe two. Or I might be there a day and leave for Zurich—I have hotel suites in a dozen cities. I'm with you today, but it might be six months before I can see you again. How can I build a relationship on that? How can I ask a woman to wait for me without being able to tell her when I'll see her again?"

"It's really quite hopeless, isn't it?" Her voice was choked, the futility swamping her.

He released her hand with controlled irritation, pausing a second before he resumed eating the rest of his breakfast. "Sometimes I forget that it is, but the inn reminds me . . . every month when I see the name on the report."

"That's why you said you didn't want an heir—that it was time the Canfield name died," she said, suddenly understanding.

"No one should have this responsibility unless he wants it," Brock stated.

"You. . . you could sell?" Stephanie suggested hesitantly.

"This is what I was trained for—what I'm good at." His mouth slanted in a half smile. "I doubt if I can make you understand that. I wouldn't change my life and what I do, even if I had the choice." He wiped at his mouth with a napkin. "That was a very good breakfast. Is there more coffee?"

"Yes, of course." A little numb, Stephanie stood up to take his cup. After all he had explained, she was still trying to figure out where she might fit into his life.

Brock must have read the bewilderment in her eyes, because he reached out to stop her when she started to pass his chair, his hand resting lightly on her forearm. "When I find something I want, I reach out and grab it, Stephanie, because it might not be there the next time I come back. I live hard and fast—and I love the same way. If I forget to say you're beautiful or that your eyes are the color of the morning sky, it isn't because I don't think of it. I just don't waste precious time.''

"Yes, I—'' Her reply was interrupted by a knock at the front door. It startled her until she realized who it was. "It's Mrs. Hammermill.''

"The egg lady,'' Brock nodded, and dropped his hands to leave Stephanie free to answer the door.

Setting his cup down, she walked toward the living room. "Yes! Come in, Mrs. Hammermill!'' she called, and the front door opened to admit a short, stout woman in a dark pillbox hat. Two dozen eggs were balanced under one short arm.

"I'm sorry I'm late, but the mister's been sick with the flu. I've been doin' his chores as well as my own.''

"I hope he's feeling better soon,'' Stephanie murmured and led the way into the kitchen. The woman stopped short at the sight of a strange man and eyed him suspiciously. Stephanie quickly introduced them.

Mrs. Hammermill was instantly all smiles. "Maybe you can talk to Perry about letting me supply the eggs for the restaurant. I would have to buy some more layers, but—''

"I'll talk to him about it,'' Brock assured her.

Taking the egg money out of the jar on the

counter, Stephanie paid the woman and tactfully hurried her on her way. She almost regretted identifying Brock, but the gossip about a strange man would have been worse.

After she had shown the woman out, Stephanie returned to the kitchen. "I'm sorry Mrs. Hammermill tried to persuade you to let her have the egg account at the restaurant inn," she apologized to Brock with a wry smile. "What she really wants Perry to do is finance it. She would have to buy more laying hens, which means she'd need to build a new coop, as well as the initial cost of more grain. She's a marvelous, dependable woman, but I don't think you want to go into partnership in the egg business." At the table she stopped to stack the dishes and add them to those in the sink waiting to be washed.

"You're right, I'm not interested in the chicken business—or the dishes. In fact—" Brock took hold of her hand and pulled her to his chair and onto his lap—I only have one merger on my mind—the one with you."

Off-balance by the move, Stephanie was dependent on the supporting steel of his arms. There was a wild flutter of her pulse as he made a sound under his breath, almost like a groan. Her hands encircled his neck, fingers seeking the vibrant thickness of his dark hair.

The kiss was sensual and exploring, their mouths mating in delighted discovery; the slow, heady joy of it insulating Stephanie from all thought. In the hard cradle of his lap, she felt the burning imprint of his thighs beneath her, the flatness of his stomach and muscled breadth of his chest and shoulders. So male, so virile! It stirred her already disturbed senses.

As he kissed her, Brock mouthed her lips and cheek, the angle of her jaw and the hollow under her ear, setting afire the urgent yearning of her body. Arousing as his kisses were, she was stimulated by the chance to let her lips wander intimately over his smooth jaw and cheek, tangy with the astringent flavor of after-shave. It was a wildly novel experience to have this freedom to reciprocate the sensuous exploration.

His caressing hands became impatient with the thick, loose folds of the large sweat shirt she was wearing. When he lifted the hem to expose her bare midriff, Stephanie drew in a breath of startled surprise that was never quite completed. Her flesh tensed under the initial touch of his hand, then melted at its firm caress.

He seemed intent on personally exploring every naked inch of her ribs and shoulders. She was quivering, her white breasts straining against the lacy material of the confining bra. When he covered one with his palm, there was a rushing release of tension that was wildly gratifying.

Yet, as his fingers sought the back fastener of her bra, sanity returned a fragment at a time. She had let herself be carried away without knowing for certain it was what she wanted. She drew away from him, pressing her hands against his chest for breathing space while she tried to clear her head of this heart-pounding passion.

"Stephanie." His voice both coaxed and commanded as he planted a kiss on an exposed shoulder bone.

"No." She gulped in the negative and swung off his lap, taking a couple of quick steps away from his chair while she pulled her sweat shirt down to her hips. "The first time I saw you, I knew I had to keep both feet on the ground or you'd knock me right off of them. I should have meant that literally." Stephanie laughed, shakily, trying to make a joke out of it even though she knew it was the absolute truth.

"I want you, Stephanie. I told you that last night," Brock reminded her. And Stephanie walked to the kitchen counter, keeping her back to him, in a weak attempt to escape the heady seduction of his voice. "If anything, it's more true at this moment."

At the scrape of the chair leg indicating he had

risen, she grabbed hold of the edge of the counter, needing to hang on to something. "It's all happening too fast for me," she tried to explain without sounding as desperate as she felt. "You don't understand, Brock. I can't be as casual about sex as you are."

"How much do you know about sex, Stephanie?" When he spoke, she realized he was directly behind her, his tone steady with patience and confidence.

Her knuckles were white from gripping the counter edge in an effort to keep from turning around. If she did, she knew she would be lost.

To counter his sureness, she became sharp and defensive. "I'm sure I don't know as much as you do, Mr. Canfield."

"Mr. Canfield?" His voice was dangerously low. His fingers gripped her shoulders and forced her to turn around. She was rigid in his hold, but she didn't resist him. Under the narrowed regard of his gray eyes, her head was thrown warily back. "Hey, what is this?" Brock demanded.

"Sex is just a physical act to you, like kissing. I don't treat it that lightly," she defended her hesitation and uncertainty.

He studied every particle of her expression for such a long time that she felt herself growing hot.

"Are you a virgin, Stephanie?" He seemed to doubt the accuracy of his conclusion.

Her gaze fell to the neckline of his sweater. "Should I apologize for my inexperience?" The challenge was a little angry, a little hurt and a little defiant.

"How old are you?" His fingers dug into the flesh of her shoulders.

"Twenty-two," she answered stiffly.

"My God, where have you been all your life? In a convent?" Brock was dryly incredulous and mocking. "Twenty-year-old virgins went out with hula hoops."

His remark ignited her temper. "It's too bad if you think I'm an oddity. My father's skiing accident left him almost completely paralyzed. I had to feed him, bathe him, dress him, read to him, do everything for him, for five years. Daddy never complained for himself, but he used to cry because I didn't go out and have fun. Perry took care of him whenever he was home, but he never knew when an emergency would come up and he'd have to go to the inn. I dated now and then." She was angry and didn't attempt to conceal it. "But who wants to get serious about someone with a sick father? We couldn't afford to hire anyone to take care of him full time. I'm not complaining about those five years. I don't regret a single one of them, because they brought me closer to my father than I'd ever been. So you can make fun of me if you want—''

He covered her mouth with two fingers to check the indignant tirade. His chiseled male features were etched in sober lines. ''I'm not making fun of you.'' He traced the outline of her mouth and became absorbed with the shape of it. Her anger vanished as if it had never been. ''It's simply rare to meet someone with your passionate nature who hasn't been around. It doesn't change anything.'' His gaze lifted to catch her look and hold it. The dark silver glitter of his eyes dazzled her. ''I'm going to keep trying to get you into bed. Knowing I would be the first just makes you a prize I'm more determined to have.''

Very slightly, his fingers tilted her chin. Then his mouth closed onto hers in consummation of his promise. A fluttering surge of desire rose within her, like a slow-burning flame fanned to burn hotter.

Brock gathered her into his arms, unhurriedly, arching her backward, his hips pinning her to the counter. The wayward caress of his hands was keenly pleasurable. He shifted his attention to the pulse quivering so wildly in her throat.

''Whose sweat shirt is this?'' he muttered when a hand became tangled in the loose folds.

"Perry's." It was a husky admission, shattered by her vivid awareness of his stark masculinity.

"*This* has got to go." He pulled at a shoulder inseam, saying the words against her neck, punctuating them with kisses. "From now on, if you wear a man's clothes, they're going to be mine."

"Whatever you say," she whispered with a throbbing ache in her voice, boneless and pliant in his arms, her forehead resting weakly against his shoulder while he rained havoc on the sensitive skin of her neck and throat.

"You know what I say." Brock seized on the submissive response, his tone fiercely low and urgent. "I've been saying it every time I looked at you or touched you. I want to make love to you—here and now. You have both feet on the floor. What do you want?"

But it wasn't that simple. Not for Stephanie. Not even with the twisting, churning rawness knotting her insides. The awful confusion kept her from answering him, but he must have felt her stillness and chose not to press the point. Instead he loosened his arms, letting his hands move in a series of restless caresses over her shoulders.

"I've postponed everything until after lunch so we could spend the morning together," he informed her in a slightly thick voice. "But there isn't any way I'm going to be able to stay in this house alone with you and not . . . ." He took a deep breath and released her entirely. "We'd better go for a drive somewhere. At least with my hands on the steering wheel, I'll be able to keep them off you. Go and change, fix yourself up—whatever you want to do. I'll wait for you down here."

Stephanie looked at him, reluctant to agree to his suggestion, but his gray eyes warned her not to protest unless she was willing to accept the alternative. That was something that still confused her.

"I'll only be a few moments," she promised.

CHAPTER FIVE

THE ROADS were crowded with the cars of tourists, eager to see the spectacle of the autumn foliage and catch a glimpse of the lore that personified Yankee New England—wooden covered bridges, white church steeples, antique shops and village squares. The route Brock took became less a planned drive and more a matter of choosing a path with the least resistance.

Stephanie relaxed in the contours of velour-covered seats, enveloped in the luxury of the blue Mercedes. The radio was turned low, its four speakers surrounding her with the serene sounds of the music. A riot of color exploded outside the window: reds and yellows against the backdrop of dark green pine forests climbing the slopes of the White Mountains, and a crisp blue sky.

Traffic thinned in the lane ahead of them as

Brock made the turn that would take them on the road south through Franconia Notch. An outcropping of granite loomed into view, and a contented smile curved Stephanie's mouth when she saw it.

"There's my friend," she murmured, unconsciously breaking the companionable silence.

"Which one?" Brock's gaze narrowed on the rear view mirror, trying to identify which of the cars they had passed that had contained her friend.

"Not that kind of friend." Her smile broadened as she pointed. "Him. The old man of the mountains." She gazed at the jagged profile Mother Nature had carved into the granite millennia ago. "I used to make up stories about him when I was a child—the way some kids do about the man in the moon, I suppose."

"If he's my only competition, I've got it made." Brock sent her a sidelong glance that was warm and desiring, beneath its teasing glitter.

"At least your heart isn't made of stone like his." They had passed the granite profile, immortalized so long ago by Nathaniel Hawthorne in his classic "The Great Stone Face." Stephanie settled back into her seat again, letting her gaze roam to Brock's profile, much more virilely alive and vigorous. Just to look at him made her feel warm. "When I was little, I was certain there was a way that I could make him come to life, some magic I could perform the way the fairy godmothers did with their enchanted wands. And he would tell me all the secrets of the world.'' She laughed softly at her whimsy.

''Now?'' Brock sounded curious, speculative.

Stephanie shrugged. ''I grew up, I guess.''

''No. All you have to do is touch me and I come to life.'' His low delivery was heavy with its sexy intonation, repeated by the languid yet serious gleam of his look. ''I can prove it whenever you want.''

Swallowing, Stephanie glanced away, feeling the feverish rise of heat in her veins. Her gaze made a restless sweep outside the window at the passing scenery, seeking escape without wanting to find it. The interior of the luxury car seemed suddenly very small and intimate. The click of the turning signals startled her, pulling her gaze to Brock.

''I think we could both use some air,'' he offered by way of explanation.

Before they reached the end of the mountain pass, he turned off and parked at the visitors' lot to the flume. When he switched off the motor, Stephanie opened the passenger door, not waiting for him to walk around the car to do it for her. The invigorating briskness of the autumn air immediately cleared her head, freeing her senses to notice other things around her.

As she waited for Brock to join her, she zipped the front of her Eisenhower jacket—a combination of dyed white and gray rabbit fur and tan leather. The legs of her deep burgundy corduroys were tucked into her high boots. The short jacket added to her clean-limbed look. The air was cool enough to turn her breath into a frosty vapor.

When Brock reached automatically for her bare hand, she automatically placed it in his, the warmth and firmness of his grip filling her with a pleasant sensation of belonging. He crooked her a faint smile before setting off to join the band of tourists lining up to get on the bus that would take them to the flume.

The endless chatter of the tourists negated the need for them to talk. Stephanie didn't mind. It left her free to savor the sensation of being squeezed close to Brock on the bus seat so a third passenger would have a place to sit.

His arm was around her, her shoulder resting against the unbuttoned front of his parka; the muscled length of his thigh and hip imprinted on her own. There was safety in the knowledge that she was surrounded by people, allowing her to simply enjoy the closeness with the temptation removed to take it to a more intimate degree.

As the bus slowed in approach of their destination, Brock murmured in her ear, "If you turn out to be a damned tease, I'm going to wring your lovely neck—after I take a bite of it.''

Her head pivoted sharply in alarm. She looked up, relieved to see he was smiling. The remark had been aimed to let her know he was deriving his own kind of pleasure from having her body crushed to his side. He lightly brushed his lips across the wing of her eyebrow in a fleeting kiss.

An older woman behind them twittered in a whisper to her companion. ''Isn't it wonderful—a pair of lovers!'' Which deepened the corners of Brock's mouth without curving them. Stephanie glanced to the front, feeling a little self-conscious.

When the bus stopped to let them out, neither of them rushed to join the mass exodus. They let the other tourists hurry on ahead of them while they followed more slowly. Stephanie wasn't as comfortable with the silence between them as she had been. When Brock removed his hand from the back of her waist to button the middle buttons of his coat, she paused with him. Ahead was the railed boardwalk winding through the cool shadows of the gorge.

''It's really better to come here in the summer when it's hot,'' she said to fill the silence. ''Then you can appreciate the coolness and the shade.''

''If you want to get warm, just let me know. I'll only be too happy to oblige.'' When her gaze fell under the lazily suggestive regard of his, he reached out to lace his fingers through her chestnut hair, pulling her toward him and lightly stroking her cheek and his other hand. He smiled gently. "You don't know how to handle all this sexual bantering, do you?"

"I've never been with anyone . . . who alludes to it as constantly as you do," she admitted, trying not to be embarrassed.

"I'm just saying what's on my mind," Brock stated, gazing deep into her blue eyes. "On my mind every time I'm near you." The vibrancy of his low voice caught at her breath, cutting it off in her throat. "Does that disturb you?"

"Yes."

"I'm glad." It was said gently, his mouth swooping down to feel the coolness of her lips against his own. Straightening, Brock took his hand away and wrapped an arm around her shoulders to turn her toward the boardwalk.

They entered the deep ravine in silence, walking side by side until the boardwalk narrowed and Stephanie moved ahead. On both sides of them, a sheer rock wall towered upward to seventy feet in the air. Moss grew thickly on the moist rock, hugging the striated crevices. In the spring and summer, delicate and rare mountain flowers blossomed in the shadowy darkness of the gorge.

A laughing stream tumbled over the rock bed running alongside and below the boardwalk. The long chasm was carved by nature and the swift waters of the Pemigewasset River, centuries before the glaciers of the Ice Age moved across the land.

The cool temperature and the high humidity combined to pierce the bones with a chilling dampness. Stephanie shoved her hands deep into the pockets of her jacket to protect them from the numbing cold. They strolled along the boardwalk that twisted and curved with the ravine. Red and gold leaves swirled downward from the trees high overhead to float in the little stream like colorful toy boats.

Stephanie paused near the end of the flume where the boardwalk made a right angle turn with the gorge. Leaning against the railing, she gazed down at the stream. A sodden group of leaves had formed a miniature dam, but the rushing water had found a spillway at one end and was fast eroding the fragile blockage.

"It's peaceful here, isn't it?" She glanced at Brock, standing beside her, leaning a hand on the railing, but it was she who had his undivided attention.

"Have dinner with me tonight, Stephanie," he said. "Just the two of us. In my suite—with wine, candlelight and soft music. I'll hire a car

and send Helen wherever the hell she wants to
go—Boston, New York, Rome. We'll have the
whole night and top it off with breakfast in bed
tomorrow morning.''

Stephanie made to move away from him, but
Brock blocked the attempt, shifting his position
to trap her to the rail, a hand on either side of
her. ''I met you less than twenty-four hours ago,''
she reasoned helplessly.

When he began brushing kisses over her neck
and cheek, Stephanie didn't resist this persuasive
tactic of a master. She was conscious of the
warmth of his breath and coolness of his mouth
against her skin, making her tingle with awareness.

''Pretend that when we met yesterday afternoon, it was two weeks ago. Dinner was a week
ago and this morning was yesterday. Time is
something I don't have in quantity. We have to
make the most of what's available, not waste it
on all these needless preliminaries,'' Brock murmured. ''Stay with me. We'll have all night to
get to know each other—in every way there is.''

She shuddered with exquisite longing and drew
back, tossing her head in a wary kind of defiance.
''You don't understand, Brock.'' Her voice was
tight and soft. ''I want to be more than a virgin
you slept with one October in New Hampshire.''

His look became stony as he straightened from

the railing. "All right," he said grimly. "Forget about tonight." His balled fists sought the pockets of his jacket, facing her with nearly a foot between them. "I have to leave shortly after noon tomorrow. What are you doing in the morning?"

The question caught Stephanie off guard. "I . . I usually go to church."

The muscles along his jawline tautened, flexing in suppressed anger. There was a bleakness in his gray eyes that chilled her with its wintry blast. "I suppose you're going to ask me to come with you. My God, Stephanie, I'd be sitting in that pew lusting after you," he expelled the words in a rush of hot anger. "Please, spare me the hypocrisy of that!"

Her mouth opened but she couldn't find anything to say. His hand snaked out to grab her elbow and propel her along the boardwalk. The serenely quiet and peaceful ravine suddenly became rife with raw tension.

Not a word was exchanged until they had returned to the car and Brock started the motor. "Will I see you before you leave?" Stephanie risked a glance at his forbidding profile as she asked the subdued question.

"Not tonight. I haven't got that kind of control."

He didn't even look at her as he reversed out of the parking space. Before he turned onto the road, he let the car idle and glanced at her. There was a softening in the hardness of his expression—a surfacing patience that was reluctant.

"We'll get together in the morning . . . before church. In the meantime—" he pushed back the sleeve of his parka to see his watch "—it's time I was back at the inn. Perry and I have an appointment to meet the architect at one."

At the farmhouse, Brock didn't bother to get out of the car. When he looked at her, not moving, Stephanie leaned across the seat to kiss him. His hands didn't touch her and his response to the contact of her lips was severely checked, barely warm.

Vaguely dejected, Stephanie walked to the house and paused at the door of the two-story brick structure to watch Brock drive away. She didn't really blame him for his attitude, but she knew that hers was not without justification, too.

ON SUNDAY morning, Stephanie awakened earlier than usual. Since Brock hadn't given her any indication when he might call or come, she didn't take the chance of being caught unaware. She was dressed complete with makeup when she went downstairs to make coffee and get the Sunday newspaper the paperboy had delivered to their doorstep.

Before she drank her second cup of coffee, she

was on pins and needles waiting for the phone to ring or the sound of a car driving up the lane. All the while the knowledge that Brock would be leaving at noon and she didn't have any idea when he would come back kept preying on her mind. A noise in the living room sent her rushing out of the kitchen, certain she had missed hearing Brock's car, but it was a bleary-eyed Perry who had caused the sound.

"Brrr, it's cold in here! Why haven't you started the fire?" he grumbled, and shivered in his corduroy robe. His hair was mussed from the night's sleep and a pair of old slippers covered his large feet as he moved tiredly toward the Count Rumford fireplace. "You're up and dressed very early this morning. How come?" He waved aside the question, kneeling to set dried logs on the grate. "I remember. You told me at supper that Brock was supposed to come over this morning."

"Yes, he is." While her brother got the fire going, Stephanie walked to the front window to look out. "You were late coming home last night."

"I know. I hope you have the coffee made," he sighed. "Is the Sunday paper here yet?" The fire was crackling merrily in the fireplace, already chasing out the chill in the room.

"Yes, to both. I'll bring them to you," she volunteered, and retraced her steps to the kitchen to pour a cup of coffee for her brother and bring him the newspaper.

When she returned, he was stretched out in his favorite armchair, his feet on the footstool, his eyes closed. She set his coffee on the lampstand beside him and dropped the paper on his lap. Perry stirred, slowly opening one eye and yawning.

"Why didn't you sleep longer?" Stephanie chided. "There wasn't any reason for you to get up this early." Sundays were, theoretically, his days off, except in the winter, but he usually stopped by the inn in the afternoons.

"I'm really bushed," he admitted. "But I woke up and couldn't go back to sleep."

While he sipped at the steaming hot coffee, Stephanie wandered to the hooked rug covering the wide floorboards in front of the fireplace. The living room was large and open, with exposed beams and hand-planed wainscoting. The sliding glass doors were decorated with October frost, partially concealing the hills rising behind the house.

"I always think I'm doing well until I come away from a meeting with Brock." Which was where Perry had been the night before until well after midnight. "Now, I feel drained and empty. He's like a sponge, absorbing everything I know out of my brain and asking endless questions," he sighed.

"About what?" Stephanie turned to study her brother, wondering if Brock had asked about her.

Perry started to answer, then interrupted her look. "No, he didn't ask about you. Obviously you told him that I gave up graduate school in law when dad had his accident."

"Why? What did he say?"

"A lot of nonsense about night school and summer courses." His mouth tightened grimly. "Which would take me forever, plus there's the problem of commuting back and forth and keeping the inn operating the way it should. No, it just isn't possible."

"What else did you talk about?" They had discussed the possibility of Perry resuming his education many times, always with the same conclusion, so Stephanie didn't argue with him now. She was too eager for any snippet of information about Brock.

"Everything from the difficulty of getting and keeping good help to renovating the whole place and turning it into the most famous ski lodge on the continent." Her brother paused, appearing to consider something. "You know, Stephanie, most of the time I feel like I'm a pretty experienced guy, but last night, in his suite, he was getting calls from half the world. My whole life is centered around that inn, yet I doubt very seriously if the inn earns enough money to pay his travel expenses for a year. I represent pretty small potatoes to his organization. The place could burn down and he'd never miss it.''

"Why are you thinking like that?" It didn't sound like her brother: his attitude was defeated and inferior.

"I don't know.'' She shrugged and sighed. "Maybe I'm jealous. Hell, I know I am,'' he laughed shortly. "There I am sitting in his suite last night, trying desperately to concentrate on the discussion, and this chick of his keeps waltzing in and out of the bedroom dressed in this sheer lacy peignoir. I spent more time imagining . . . .'' Perry stopped at the sight of the ashen color that spread over Stephanie's face. "I'm sorry. Stephanie, don't be a fool.''

"Please, don't say anything,'' she protested softly. "There isn't anything you can say that I haven't told myself already.'' She turned, needing a few minutes by herself. "Excuse me. I'm going to get some coffee.''

When she returned to the living room, Perry was buried in the front page of the newspaper, and the conversation wasn't resumed. Stephanie sat on the sofa to drink her coffee. The minute it was gone she was up, walking to the window to look at the empty scene. Back and forth she went—too nervous to stay seated, while the grandfather clock ticked away the minutes.

"A watched pot never boils," Perry remarked on her tenth trip to the window.

"I know it." She walked to the fireplace to add another log to the waning fire.

"It's getting late," he observed. "I'd better get dressed for church. Are you coming?"

Rising, she glanced toward the window. "I . . . ." Then Stephanie saw the blue Mercedes coming up the drive. "He's here!"

She dashed to the door and was outside by the time Brock stepped from the car. Her smile froze into place when she spied the blonde sitting in the passenger seat. Her gaze swung in hurt confusion back to Brock as he approached, his features grimly drawn.

"I have to leave. With luck, I'll make it to New York in time to catch the afternoon flight to Geneva," he said.

Stephanie couldn't speak, her throat paralyzed. She could only stare at him with her rounded blue eyes. The frosty chill of the October morning wasn't nearly as cold as she felt. He was leaving, and they wouldn't even have the morning together.

"I came to say goodbye," Brock continued. "I should have called, but . . . ." His jaw hardened. "I told you this could happen. Dammit,

I warned you!'' He grabbed her by the shoulders as if to shake her.

The physical pain was almost welcome. In the next second, he was yanking her into his arms and bruising her lips with a hard, angry kiss, relentless in its punishment. But his savagery aroused an emotion stronger than pain. It engulfed her, leaving her weak and breathless when he broke the contact.

He pushed her away and had already turned to walk to the car before he muttered a rather final sounding, ''Goodbye, Stephanie.''

But she couldn't get that one word out—not even his name. The car had been started and was turning around. Still Stephanie hadn't moved from where he'd left her at the door.

There was no last glance from Brock—no wave, nothing. Tears misted over her eyes, blinding her vision. She didn't see the exact moment when his car disappeared from view down the long lane.

Entering the house, she was aware of Perry's blurred outline near the stairwell. ''He had to leave . . . for Geneva.'' Her voice was choked and very small Her brother looked at her for a long minute, but didn't say anything as he turned to climb the stairs. Stephanie walked blindly into the kitchen where she cried slow, silent tears.

THE NORTH WINDS came to strip the leaves from the trees, exposing the dark skeletons of the trunks and leaving piles of brown leaves to carpet the ground. The first snow flurry of the season came the last weekend in October. November arrived.

Stephanie had written Brock two letters, short ones with news of the inn and the area, minus any personal messages. The only address she had was the one the monthly reports were sent to. She couldn't be sure if they would reach him. Last week, she had sent merely a postcard.

There hadn't been a single reply of any kind, and she was gradually becoming convinced he had forgotten her. She couldn't shake the feeling that she had been on the brink of discovering something wonderful, only to lose it.

The ring of her office extension drew a sigh. Unclipping an earring, she answered the phone. "Miss Hall speaking. May I help you?"

"How are you?" a familiar male voice inquired.

Incredulous, Stephanie tightened her grip on the receiver, the blood singing in her veins. "Brock?" She could feel her voice choking. "Where are you?" In the background she could hear a hum of voices.

"Can you believe it?" His short laugh was a quietly harsh sound. "I'm in the middle of a board meeting. I don't know who the hell they think I'm talking to, but I had to call you.''

''I'm glad.'' Her answer was hardly above a whisper.

''The mail packet caught up with me this morning. I got the letter and postcard you sent,'' he said.

''I . . . I wasn't sure if I should write,'' she admitted.

''These are liberated times, but I'm not surprised that you're behind them,'' he mocked, but not unkindly.

A voice intruded from the background. ''Mr. Canfield, here's the breakdown report you wanted on the foreign currency exchange this quarter.''

''Good, Frank,'' was Brock's partially muffled response, then clearer, ''Are you still there?''

''Yes, I'm here,'' Stephanie assured him, her voice regaining its strength.

Brock started to say something, then changed his mind. ''This is the most frustrating means of communication.'' His tone was low and charged with irritation. ''I can't see you or touch you.''

''I know.'' There was a certain torment in hearing his voice.

''Mr. Canfield?'' The same voice interrupted Brock again.

''Dammit, Frank, can't you see I'm on the phone?'' he demanded. He came back on the line, sighing tiredly. "I'm sorry. It's no good, I can't talk now. I'm trying to schedule a trip there in December or January."

That long, Stephanie thought, but didn't say it. Instead she attempted a light remark. "The heart of the skiing season. Maybe you'll have enough time to spend an afternoon on the slopes. We already have a good snow cover."

"I don't give a damn about the snow." He controlled the impatience in his voice to add a promising, "I'll see you . . . soon, I hope."

"Goodbye, Brock."

The line clicked dead before Stephanie hung up the phone. She stared at it until a flicker of movement caught her attention and she looked up to see Perry in the doorway.

"Was that Brock?" He studied her quietly.

"Yes." She reclipped the earring on her lobe, unwilling to discuss the sweetly short conversation with Brock.

A sadness stole into his features. "Don't let him break your heart, Steph." His hand slapped at the doorjamb in a helpless gesture as he turned to walk down the hallway to his office.

CHAPTER SIX

THERE WEREN'T any more calls from Brock. Stephanie continued to write him, but not more frequently than she had before. Other than to say she looked forward to his next trip to New Hampshire, she didn't make any possessive references to him. She knew that the next time she saw him it might all be different, and she didn't want any potentially embarrassing letters sent by her.

The forecast for Thanksgiving called for snow. It was falling steadily in fat flakes, accumulating quickly on a ground that was white from previous snowfalls. It was a workday as usual, the Thanksgiving holiday weekend being one of their biggest of the winter season.

When Stephanie entered the kitchen that morning, her brother was at the big door, bundling up with boots, muffler and gloves. ''Let's forget about breakfast this morning. I'm going out to put the snow chains on the wagon. We'll eat when we get to the inn.''

"When the weatherman said snow last night, he meant it, didn't he?'' She glanced out of the frosty window at the large flakes veiling the gray white hills.

"We're in for a storm,'' Perry prophesied. "It wouldn't hurt if you grabbed a clean shirt and my shaving kit, and something for yourself. If this keeps up, we'll just sleep at the inn tonight. Our road is always the last one the snowplows hit.'' He grimaced and ducked out the back door amid a whirl of snowflakes and cold air.

The drive from the farmhouse to the inn usually took ten minutes, but the limited visibility and the slippery roads caused by the falling snow increased it to twenty-five. The car radio forecast worsening conditions.

Before breakfast was over the area slopes were closed to skiers. The inn suddenly seemed more crowded than usual because all the guests were virtually confined to the inn. They congregated in the lobby around the fireplace, the games room, the lounge and the restaurants. There was even a line to use the recently completed sauna and exercise room. Almost any flat surface was commandeered for a game of cards. Impromptu chess and checkers tournaments were held.

Shortly after twelve noon there was a mild panic when it was discovered that two cross-country skiers hadn't reported in from an overnight trip. Perry and Stephanie had just sat down to the restaurant's turkey dinner. The adventurers were finally located at another lodge, but their dinners were cold when they returned to them.

Then the deluge of stranded motorists began. Although they were full, Stephanie temporarily doubled up rooms where she could, shifting all the members of one family into a room, helped housekeeping figure out how many spare blankets, sheets, cots and pillows were on hand and how many motorists they could handle, and filled in wherever else she was needed.

"Don't forget to save us a place to sleep," Perry reminded her at one point when she was working out the capacity of the sofas in the lobby.

"There's always the floor," she retorted with a laugh.

It was almost a relief when the storm knocked the telephone lines out late in the afternoon and the switchboard finally stopped buzzing. The dinner hour didn't bring a letup in the frantic pace. With all the extra people, both Perry and Stephanie lent a hand in the restaurant kitchen, doing everything from helping to fix the food to running the dishwasher.

At nine-thirty Perry laid a hand on her shoulder.

"You've done enough, Steph. Why don't you call it a night?"

"Yessir, boss," she agreed readily. "What about you?"

"I'm going to the lounge. Freddie needs some help behind the bar. And—" he breathed in tiredly "—I'd better be around in case someone gets rowdy."

Stephanie was tempted to insist he let someone else do it, but Perry took his responsibility as manager too seriously to shrug it onto someone else. "Okay, I'll see you in the morning."

"Wait a minute!" He called her back when she started to turn away. "Where do I sleep tonight?"

"On the couch in your office . . . unless it's already occupied," she joked. "In that event, you're on your own."

"Thanks a lot, sis," he retorted in a mock growl.

Stopping at her office, Stephanie picked up the small overnight bag she had packed and started down the hallway. She didn't know which sounded more divine—a shower or sleep? With luck, she would be able to have both.

Before she knocked at the door of the suite, she heard the childish giggles coming from in side. Her knocks produced some shrieks and more giggles. The door was opened by a young woman, barely a year older than Stephanie. She looked tired, harassed and exasperated, her smile growing thin.

"Hi. It's me, your roommate for the night." Stephanie struggled to sound cheerful.

"Of course, come in, Miss Hall." But she was diverted by the impish little five-year-old girl who appeared in the connecting doorway to the bedroom. "Amy Sue, you get back in that bed before I spank you!" the woman threatened, and the little nightgowned figure fled in laughter. "I'm sorry. I've been trying to get the girls asleep for the last hour. They think this is some kind of a party."

"It's all new. They're just excited, Mrs. Foster. And please, call me Stephanie," she insisted.

"I'm Madge." She walked to the bedroom. "And these are my daughters, Amy, five, and Marsha, four."

Amy, the oldest, quickly scurried under the covers. The king-sized bed seemed to swallow up the two small girls with their dark hair. The pair eyed Stephanie with bold curiosity.

"Hello, Amy and Marsha," she smiled. The two looked anything but sleepy with their bright brown eyes.

"Hello. Who are you?" The youngest asked,

exhibiting no shyness because Stephanie was a stranger.

"My name is Stephanie," she replied.

"My friend in day care has that same name," Amy piped.

"Will you read us a story?" Marsha dived for the storybooks on the nightstand beside the bed. "Read mine."

"No, mine!" Amy protested.

"Girls!" Madge Foster attempted to intervene with some measure of authority.

"I don't mind," Stephanie murmured. "I'll read to them while you relax in the tub." When the woman hesitated, obviously tempted, Stephanie repeated, "Really, I don't mind."

"Thank you. I don't know what to say," the woman faltered. "All day long, trying to drive in that storm, with those girls bouncing all over, then being stranded here . . . my nerves could use a rest. But I won't leave them with you for long, I promise."

"Read my story, please?" Amy pleaded.

"I'll read them both," Stephanie promised. "But we'll start with Marsha's first."

She set her overnight case on the floor by the bed and walked over to sit on the edge where the bedside lamp was lit. Marsha immediately pressed her book into Stephanie's hands. They grumbled when she insisted that they had to crawl under the covers and lie down before she would read to them. They didn't give in until she had agreed to show them the pictures on each page.

Her ploy worked. By the time she had read the first story for the third time, both girls had fallen asleep. When the bathroom door opened Stephanie held a silencing finger to her lips. Madge Foster smiled and shook her head in disbelief.

"You must have my husband Ted's kind of voice. I can read until I'm hoarse, but they go right to sleep for him," she whispered. "I don't think my head is even going to have a chance to touch the pillow before I'm asleep. The bathroom is all yours, and it's like heaven."

"Good." Stephanie flexed her shoulders as the fatigue began to set in. She picked up her night case and started toward the marble bathroom.

"Oh, Miss H . . . Stephanie, do you mind if I leave the lamp burning on my side of the bed? The girls don't like to sleep in the dark. I've been trying to break them of it, but this is a strange place and . . . if it wouldn't bother you. . .?"

"No, it won't bother me. I'm like you," Stephanie explained. "I'll probably be asleep before my head's on the pillow."

"The girls don't toss and turn very much, so I don't think they'll disturb you."

"I'm sorry we weren't able to provide you with a room of your own," Stephanie apologized.

"Listen, I'm just grateful for a bed to sleep in. And heaven knows, this one is big enough to hold two more," Madge smiled. "Go and take your bath. And good night."

"Yes, good night."

The hot bath water made Stephanie realize how mentally and physically exhausted she was. It was an effort to towel dry and pull on her night-dress. All three were asleep when she reentered the bedroom. She moved quietly to the far side of the bed on the fringe of the pool of light cast by the lamp. She, too, drifted into sleep within minutes.

A coolness roused her, a vague sensation of a draft. Stephanie tried to pull the covers tighter around her neck, but something held them down. She started to turn onto her side, only to become conscious of something heavy weighing the edge of the mattress down.

Her lashes opened to a narrow slit, then widened at the outline of a person sitting on the bed beside her. It was a full second before she realized who the man in the white shirt was.

"Brock!" Was she dreaming? She said his name softly in case she scared his image away.

But his hand touched her face in a light, cool caress and she knew it wasn't a dream. "Hello."

"What are you doing here?" she breathed, keeping her voice low.

He looked tried and drawn: she could see that in the half-light from the lamp. But the glint in his gray eyes was anything but weary.

"Here you are finally in my bed, and there isn't room for me." His gaze danced to the sleeping children in the center of the bed, their faces illuminated by the soft glow spilling from the lamp.

"The storm—" Stephanie started to explain in a whisper.

"Yes, I know. I stepped over bodies in the lobby." Without warning, Brock straightened to fold back the covers and slide his arms beneath her, picking her up.

Stephanie clutched at his neck, too stunned and sleepy to struggle and too conscious of the possibility of waking the children or their mother. "What are you doing, Brock?" The question was issued in confused excitement, her pulse accelerating at this contact with his leanly muscled frame.

"I'm taking you into the other room with me," he stated, and carried her through the connecting door to the sitting room. "We have an hour of Thanksgiving left and I mean to spend it with you."

Brock didn't put her down until they were inside the room and the door was shut. A single light burned in the far corner. Outside the window the snow was still falling, but slower and not as thickly as it had been earlier.

Not quite able to believe he was really there in the flesh, Stephanie gazed at his manly features, the darkness of his hair and the melting grayness of his eyes. His hands encircled her waist, gliding over the silken material of her nightgown to bring her slowly closer as if he enjoyed the feel of her.

When his mouth began a downward movement toward her, Stephanie went on tiptoes to meet it. He took possession of the yielding softness of her lips with a gentle sensuality. It was so different from any other kiss that she could hardly understand what was happening to her.

His hands were at the small of her back, caressing but firm against her silk-covered skin and holding her close to the hardening contours of his thighs. Her blood ran with fire as he practiced the subtle art of seduction so expertly and so effortlessly. Stephanie was lost to his skill and she didn't care. When at last he released her lips to seek the bareness of a shoulder, she sighed her enchanted contentment. It gradually dawned on her that the coolness she was feeling against her scantily clad body did not come from any draft in the room. It was Brock who was chilled.

"You're cold," she murmured in concern.

"So?" His mouth was against her ear, his tongue circling its sensitive hollows. "Warm me up."

Taking him literally at his word, Stephanie pressed closer to him in an effort to warm him with her body heat. "How did you get here in this storm?" she asked, her mouth brushing the coolness of his shirt at his shoulder. "I still can't believe you're really here," she sighed at the miracle of being in his arms.

"Neither can I!" His arms tightened fiercely for an instant. "There were times when I wondered whether I would make it," he admitted in a tired and rueful sigh.

"Why did you come? With this storm and all. . .?" Stephanie lifted her head, shuddering when she thought of him out there in that blizzard. She was frightened by what might have happened. Her hand glided along the smoothness of his jaw and he rubbed his cheek into her palm.

"Why did you take such a risk?" Her voice was choked by the dangerous chance he had taken.

"I wanted to be with you." He gazed deep into her eyes, letting his look add a heady force to his statement. "I didn't want to spend the holiday without you."

"You should have called. You should have let me know you were coming," Stephanie admonished, but she knew she would have been worried sick about him.

"I wanted to surprise you." His mouth twisted in a wry line. "It's been an eighteen-hour obstacle course—closed airports, diverted flights, trains not running, highways closed. When I finally admitted there was a distinct possibility I wouldn't make it, the telephone lines were down. I couldn't get through to tell you I wanted to be here."

"Brock. . . ." The frustration he had suffered was very real to her.

"I know." The circle of his arms tightened as he pressed a kiss to her temple.

"How did you get here?" She still marveled that he had actually made it.

"I rented a car and bribed a maintenance crew to let me follow their snowplow," he explained.

"How did you guess I'd be here at the inn?"

"I didn't. I went to your home first," Brock told her.

"But the lane—" Stephanie's eyes widened in alarmed protest.

"Was blocked," he finished the sentence for her. "I had to leave the car on the road and walk back to the house. It's a good thing you and Perry are the trusting sort and left the back door unlocked. When I discovered the house was empty, I guessed you'd decided to spend the night at the inn, so I came here. Of course, I never expected to find you sleeping in my bed. Lucky for me, the night clerk knew where you were bunking and I didn't have to go around knocking on doors in the middle of the night trying to find you. Perry would have had some irate guests on his hands come morning.''

She was shaken by his single-minded determination to find her, to be with her. Surely it had to mean something? Mere sexual attraction couldn't be all it was that they shared. The thought left her feeling slightly euphoric and dazed by the fiery surge of emotion rushing through her system.

''Come.'' Moving, Brock took hold of her hand and led her to the side of the room. ''I took the seat cushions off the sofa and the spare pillows and blankets from the closet to make us a bed on the floor in here.''

Stephanie stared at the blanket-covered cushions on the floor and the two pillows lying side by side at the top. Brock was studying her, waiting for her reaction. But there was none—at least, not a negative one.

''I'll turn out the light.'' Releasing her hand, Brock moved to the opposite side of the room where the lamp burned.

Stephanie watched him. There wasn't any conscious decision on her part. She was only aware of how very close she had come to losing him to the winter storm. All arguments for and against going to bed with him paled in comparison to that unshakable fact. It was truly the only thought in her mind.

When the click of a light switch buried the room in darkness, she sank onto the hard foam cushions. A sublime calmness settled through her as she folded back the blanket to slide beneath it.

She loved Brock. The quiet knowledge wasn't a rationale for her action, but the simple truth. Implausible as it seemed, as short a time as she had known him, she loved him. The unshakable strength of emotion made her feel mellow and warm, ripe with the fullness of it.

Brock was a dark shadow as he approached the makeshift bed. Not until he had joined her under the covers did he take form and substance. Lying on his side, he reached for her to draw her into his embrace.

Her hands encountered the muscled bareness of his chest, its dark hair sensually rough beneath her palms, his legs shifting to tangle with hers. The sweet intimacy twisted its knife-sharp blade into her stomach, a heady desire building.

His mouth sought and found hers, covering it with a softly bruising force and demanding a response that she had no wish to suppress. He mastered her with a fiery hunger, possessing her heart and soul, which she was only too willing to give into his keeping. With a surrendering sigh, she slid her arms around the smooth skin covering his hard shoulders to bring more of his weight onto her.

The blanket slipped to a position over their hips as Brock pushed the silken strap of her nightgown off a shoulder. His mouth explored the rose-crested top of a breast that had been exposed to his dark gray eyes. It heightened the taut desire curling her toes and knotting her insides. Then his mouth returned to crush her lips while the sensually abrasive hair on his chest brushed across the sensitive skin of her naked breast.

A moaning sound came from his throat, his warm breath filling her mouth with suffocating sweetness. The thin barrier of her nightgown didn't keep out the sensation of the growing limpness of his body.

Reluctantly, Brock drew away from her to roll onto his back, an arm flung above his head onto the pillow. Stephanie was confused and aching by this withdrawal. Turning onto her side, she levered herself onto an elbow to gaze at him.

His gaze slid to her, the vibrant glitter fading from his eyes. He reached out to slide the strap of her gown onto her shoulder, his hand remaining to silently caress her. A half smile was lifting one corner of his mouth. Even that seemed to require a lot of effort.

"What's wrong, Brock?" Stephanie asked uncertainly, wanting to curl herself into his arms, but refraining to obey the impulse because of the lack of an invitation.

"I've been working some long hours the last few days, trying to clear up any business that might come up at the last minute and kept me from coming here to be with you." His hand moved to rest on the curve of her neck beneath the curtain of chestnut hair. "I've had six hours of sleep in the last fifty-two. That's what's wrong."

She heard the weariness in his voice, but in the dimness of the darkened room she could only guess at the strain of fatigue etched in his features. When he chuckled softly, she frowned in confusion.

"Don't you see the irony of this, Stephanie?" Brock murmured. "After all this time you're finally beside me—here in this bed, just the way I imagined it. And now I'm too damned tired to do anything about it," he sighed in irritation.

Her personal dissatisfaction was forgotten in a rush of loving concern for him. Leaning forward, she kissed his lips with infinite tenderness. A loving smile curved her mouth when she straightened.

"You'd better get some sleep before you collapse,'' she advised, and turned to sweep back the covers to return to her own bed.

"No." Brock waylaid her action with an outstretched hand. "Stay with me tonight."

Her hesitation was fractional. Accepting his invitation, she lay down once more beside him. Brock turned her onto her side with her back to him and curled her against his length. His arm was around her waist, a hand possessively cupping a breast.

Stephanie was warmed by the memory that Brock had once insisted that he preferred to sleep alone. He shared this need to be close—a need that transcended every thought and feeling that might have been true in the past. What they had was unique. Stephanie knew it, and she suspected Brock did, too.

Hugged close to him, she heard his breathing grow deep and heavy as tiredness carried him quickly to sleep. She closed her eyes, not certain that she would drift off so quickly, but the utter contentment soon whisked her away. Thus they slept spoon fashion, enfolded in an embrace of passive desire.

Morning light infiltrated the room through the large windows, pricking at Stephanie's eyelids. She became conscious of a heavy weight across her legs and stomach. A delicious heat was radiating from something and she snuggled closer to it. When she realized the heartbeat she was hearing did not belong to her, she opened her eyes.

A pair of broad shoulders were in front of her, tanned skin stretched across sinewy muscles and darkened with rough, curling hairs. The weight across her stomach was Brock's arm, his hand cupped to her hipbone in firm possession, while a leg was hooked across her knees. Peering through the top of her lashes, she studied the unrelenting strength of his face in sleep. Lean and powerful, he stirred her senses.

There was a very strong impulse to kiss him awake, but the amount of sunlight streaming through the windows and the muffled voices of others in the outer hall warned Stephanie of the lateness of the hour.

Reluctantly she slid out of his hold and out of the makeshift bed on the floor. Her bare feet made no sound as she entered the bedroom where the young woman and her two children were still sleeping. With her overnight bag in hand, she slipped into the bathroom to wash and dress.

There wasn't a sound from anyone when she came out. She hesitated in the sitting room, but Brock was still sound asleep. He had left the key to his suite lying on an end table. Stephanie slipped it into her pocket and quietly left the room through the hall door.

She went directly to the restaurant kitchen. The inn was already astir with early morning breakfasters. Outside, the sky was clear—almost too blue against the pure snow white of the ground. She laid a tray with china cups and a pot of coffee to take to the suite.

As she was passing through the lobby, her brother appeared. "Stephanie!" he called out to stop her. "Brock's here," he said when he reached her side. "He arrived last night."

"Yes, I know," she nodded. "I'm taking him some coffee now. He's still sleeping. He made a bed on the floor of the sitting room." She didn't mention that she had shared it with him. It wasn't an attempt to conceal the knowledge from Perry. Rather, she preferred to choose her own time to tell him when there weren't others around who might overhear and misinterpret her action.

Perry glanced at the tray, then at her, studying her closely. "Why is he here? Did he say?" he questioned.

"He wanted to have Thanksgiving here." She hesitated over carrying the explanation further, but she needn't have.

Her brother did it for her. "With you," he identified the reason specifically.

"Yes," Stephanie nodded, unable to keep the radiance from shining in her eyes.

Perry shook his head in absent amazement.

"In that blizzard . . ." he murmured. He bit at his lip in a second of pensive silence. "Maybe I was wrong about him . . . and his interest in you," he offered. Whatever else he was about to add, he changed his mind and flashed her a wry smile. "You'd better take that coffee to him before it gets cold."

"I'll be back shortly," she promised.

"No rush," Perry insisted. "After the long day you put in yesterday, you can be as late as you want this morning."

Her smile was full of affection for her brother. "Thanks, boss."

At the door to the suite, Stephanie had to set the tray on the floor to have her hands free to unlock the door. The cups rattled on their china saucers as she entered the sitting room, but the delicate noise didn't waken Brock, who was still sleeping soundly on the floor. Only silence came from the bedroom where the young woman and her two little girls were.

Stephanie carried the tray to the rattan table and set it there. Knowing how little sleep Brock had in the last few days, she didn't pour him any coffee yet, only a cup for herself. The thermal pot would keep the coffee hot for a long time. She walked to a chair, unconsciously choosing one that would permit her to watch Brock in sleep.

The blanket was down around his hips, exposing his lean, untanned torso to her inspection. Briefly she was fascinated by the button roundness of his navel, a dark hollow in his flat stomach. He was lying on his side, facing her.

Stephanie let her gaze wander upward to his strongly defined mouth and the thickness of dark lashes resting against his cheekbone. His brows were thick and malely arched. Across his forehead was a thatch of rumpled dark hair. Even in sleep, Brock exuded an incredible virility. She wanted to touch him so much, it was almost a physical pain.

When he stirred, she unconsciously held her breath. His hand moved across the empty cushion beside him, as if instinctively seeking something. Was he in search of her? What a wondrous thought! His hand froze for a full second, then instantly he was awake, turning onto his back and alarm flashed in his expression.

"Stephanie!" He called out for her in an impatient voice a fraction of a second before he saw her seated in the chair. His expression changed immediately to one of satisfaction.

"Good morning." Her voice was husky with the knowledge that he had missed having her sleeping form beside him.

"Not so good," Brock denied her adjective

in describing the morning. "You should have awakened me when you awoke."

"Would you like some coffee?" Stephanie rose, conscious of his gaze taking in her fully dressed appearance, detail by detail. Without waiting for his acceptance, she walked to the table and poured a cup for him.

"Why did you get dressed right away?" he questioned before his gaze flickered past her to the sunlight that drenched the room. "What time is it?"

"Nearly nine o'clock." She carried the cup to him.

The blanket had slipped a little farther downward, giving her a tantalizing glimpse of the elastic waistband of his white jockey shorts. It was crazy the way her pulse reacted to the sight, yet she had entered her brother's bedroom many times to waken him when he slept through his alarm, and found him similarly clad. She hadn't even blinked an eye then.

"I suppose you have to work this morning." His mouth was grim as he looked up when she stood beside the crude bed. He was still supported by his elbows and forearms in a half-reclining position.

"No. Perry said it was okay if I was late," she assured him, and knelt down to give him his coffee.

But Brock didn't reach for it. "In that case, come back to bed." His gaze became obsessively attached to her lips, sending her heart knocking against her ribs.

Stephanie couldn't find her voice. She recovered it after he had sat up and circled one arm around her waist while his hand curved itself to the back of her neck, pulling her toward him.

"I'm going to spill the coffee," she warned a breath before his mouth covered her lips to hungrily remind her of the volatile attraction they shared.

Her hand gripped his hard shoulder for balance while the cup of coffee jiggled in its saucer in the opposite hand, the steaming liquid sloshing over the china rim. But she offered no resistance to his kiss, melting under his heady domination.

"Ged rid of that coffee and those clothes, and come back to bed with me," Brock ordered against her mouth, and proceeded to outline her lips with his tongue.

He kissed her thoroughly and sensually before drawing away. Stephanie was drugged in a euphoric state, barely capable of thought when she met the gray darkness of his eyes. A sound intruded, a mere irritation until a movement entered her vision, drawing her glance.

Five-year-old Amy was standing in the doorway wearing her flannel nightgown, one bare foot on top of the other, eyeing the pair of them curiously. Stephanie was brought sharply to her senses. Brock turned to look behind him and barely stifled a curse of frustration rather than anger. There was a glitter of ironic amusement and profound regret when he glanced back to Stephanie.

"Who's that man?" Amy wanted to know. "Is he your husband?"

Brock rescued the cup of coffee from her shaking hand and arched a mocking brow in her direction. "No, he's a friend," Stephanie explained a little self-consciously.

The little girl padded quickly across the room as if invited. "Why are you sleeping on the floor?" she asked Brock, and bounced onto the cushions to sit on a pillow with her legs under her.

"Because there wasn't any place else for me to sleep," he replied, regarding the little girl's intrusion with a patience and tolerance that faintly surprised Stephanie.

"There was lots of room in the bed," Amy insisted.

"It looked a little more crowded than I wanted." His glance darted to Stephanie, heavy with secret meaning.

A drowsy Marsha entered the room, rubbing her sleep-filled eyes and hugging her storybook in front of her. She pattered quickly to her older sister's side and curled onto the edge of the pillow, sitting cross-legged and yawning.

Brock took a sip of his coffee and murmured to Stephanie, "This bed is nearly as full as mine was last night."

"Were you going to wrestle?" the oldest brunette girl inquired innocently.

His look was amused, yet narrowed. "Why do you ask?"

"Because mommy and daddy do that sometimes in the mornings," she explained. "Daddy tickles and tickles her. It makes mommy laugh so hard she cries. Then daddy kisses her like you were doing."

"I see." The corners of his mouth deepened with the containment of a smile. "Then what happens?"

Stephanie gasped in sharp embarrassment, drawing the wicked glint of his gaze.

"Then mommy's cheeks get pink like Stephanie's are," Amy admitted with guileless charm. "She shoos us to our own rooms and helps us get dressed so we can go outside and play."

The answer didn't put Stephanie any more at ease under Brock's disturbing and mocking look. "Is your mother awake?" she asked, hoping to change the subject.

"Not yet." It was obvious it didn't matter much to either of the girls. "Do you have any children?'' Amy directed the question to Brock. Like any female, she was drawn to the male of the species.

''No,'' he replied as his gaze roamed over the two little girls.

''Wouldn't you like to have a little girl of your own?'' Amy seemed puzzled. ''Daddy says it's wonderful, especially when you have two.''

''He does, does he?'' Brock was deliberately noncommittal although he glanced almost automatically at Stephanie.

''Yes. You can have little boys, too,'' Amy hastened to add.

''But they can be mean sometimes,'' Marsha piped in for the first time. ''Jimmy Joe Barnes stepped on my doll and broke its head on purpose.''

''But daddy fixed it,'' Amy reminded her, before turning back to Brock. ''Which do you think you'd rather have?''

''I don't know. Do little boys crawl in bed with their parents in the morning, too?'' he asked with his tongue in his cheek.

''I think so.'' Amy's frown revealed she didn't understand the relevancy of that question.

''Which would you rather have, Stephanie?'' Brock eyed her with deliberate suggestiveness, stealing her breath. ''Boys or girls? Or one of each?''

"I—" She was spared from answering that provocative question by the interruption of Madge Foster's voice coming from the bedroom.

"Amy? Marsha? Where are you?" she called in sleepy alarm.

"We're in here, mommy," Amy answered immediately.

"What are you . . . ." the question was never finished as the young woman appeared in the doorway.

The sight of Brock sitting half-naked with Stephanie and her daughters made the woman suddenly and embarrassingly conscious of the revealing nightgown she was wearing. Quickly she stepped behind the door, using it as a shield.

"You girls come here right now," she ordered. "You haven't brushed your teeth yet," she added, as if that was the reason.

The pair hopped blithely to their feet and dashed into the bedroom. Madge sent Stephanie a grimacing look of apology before closing the door.

"Now—" Brock caught at Stephanie's hand to pull her off-balance and into his arms "—where were we before we were so rudely interrupted?" His mouth had barely touched her lips when there was a knock at the hall door. Releasing her, he muttered, "This place is turning into Grand Central Station. You'd better hand me my pants, there's likely to be a parade through here any minute."

Before she answered the door, Stephanie handed him the trousers draped over a nearby chair. It was one of the housekeepers doing a room check. When Stephanie turned around after closing the door, Brock was on his feet, semidecently clad in the dark pants.

"More coffee?" she suggested.

"Since circumstances don't allow anything else, why not?" he shrugged with a wry smile. She had just started to fill his cup when the telephone rang. Brock motioned her to stay where she was. "I'll get it." He answered it, then hesitated, glancing at Stephanie as he responded to the caller, "Just a minute, please." He held the mouthpiece slightly away. "The young woman occupying the bedroom—is her last name Foster?"

"Yes, it is," Stephanie nodded.

"It's her husband on the phone," he explained. "Evidently the telephones are back in service. There's an extension by the bed she can use."

"I'll tell her." She handed Brock his cup before she walked over to knock on the connecting door. "Madge, your husband is on the phone."

The delighted shrieks of the two young girls came first from the bedroom, then echoed into the sitting room through the phone in Brock's hand. He set the receiver on its cradle and let a glance slide at Stephanie.

"How do you suppose she's going to explain that a man answered?" he mocked.

"With the storm and all, I'm sure her husband will understand." She dismissed it as a problem and retrieved her coffee cup from the side table to refill it.

As he was pouring the coffee from the thermal pot, Brock came up behind her, sliding an arm around the front of her waist and bending to kiss the side of her neck. "Believe me, if I called you and a man other than your brother answered the phone, you'd have a lot of explaining to do."

A delicious tingle danced over her skin at his nibbling kisses. "I'll remember to always answer the phone myself from now on," she mocked, "especially when I'm entertaining male friends."

His arm tightened with a sudden fierceness. "I'm not joking, Stephanie. Just thinking of someone else touching you—"

Someone rapped very softly on the hall door. Brock cursed savagely as he broke away from her and crossed the room with long, impatient strides to jerk the door open.

Perry stood outside, briefly startled. "I wasn't sure if you were up yet."

Brock's laugh was a harsh sound. "I'm awake, all right. Thanks to two little girls, then their mother, then a telephone call from their father, and a housekeeper fits in the order of things somewhere. Come in—everybody else does.'' Irritation negated the attempt at humor. ''I suppose you need Stephanie.''

''Indirectly.'' Perry's gaze was ruefully apologetic when it met hers. ''I need the revised rate schedule we made yesterday afternoon. I looked on your desk, but I couldn't find it.''

''It's in the folder in the top, right-hand drawer of my desk,'' she quickly supplied its location.

''What's it like getting out of here?'' Brock demanded unexpectedly. She stared at him, not wanting to believe the implication of that question. Brock didn't even glance her way.

''The airport is closed still, but the highways are open. The snow is drifting in places, but otherwise it's in good shape, according to the highway-patrol report we got this morning,'' her brother replied.

''You aren't leaving?'' Stephanie almost accused.

''I have to.'' Then he flashed her an angry look, noting the sharp hurt in her expression. ''Dammit! I don't like it any more than you do!''

Very quietly, Perry slipped out of the room, leaving them alone. Stephanie turned away from Brock, trying to hide her bitter disappointment. She heard him set his cup down and walk up behind her. His hands settled hesitantly on her shoulders.

"Twenty-four hours was all I could spare, Stephanie," he explained grimly. "I've already used more than that, most of it trying to get here."

"I understand that." She turned and was confronted by the naked wall of his chest. Lifting her gaze she looked into his face. "Honestly, I'm glad you came . . . for however long or short it has to be."

His gray eyes no longer smoldered with a resenting anger, but burned with a sultry fire as they lingered for a long, disruptive moment on her parted lips. There was no longer any hesitation in the touch of his hands as he drew her up to meet his descending mouth.

His kiss seared her with the rawness of his hunger, arousing her to the full awareness of his need and making her ache for male aggression of his wants. Her arms wound around his neck as she was crushed willingly against his chest. Before the embrace erupted out of control, Brock set her from him with a groan.

"You'd better go now," he advised tightly. "We aren't going to have any more time alone. And I'd rather say goodbye now."

"Brock!" It was a silent protest.

"Believe me, it's better this way," he insisted. "I'll see you when I can, you know that, don't you?"

"Yes," she nodded, and tried not to think about how long that might be.

He walked her to the hall door, brushing her lips with a kiss before she left the room. Her throat was raw and her eyes burned, but she didn't cry. An inner voice warned her that these farewells were something she had better accept. They would be very numerous in any prolonged relationship with Brock Canfield.

Perry didn't say anything when she walked into her office to find him going over the schedule he had removed from her desk drawer. There was gentle sympathy in his look and a suppressed concern.

For nearly two hours she waited, clinging to the hope that Brock would stop by to see her one last time before he left. But he went without seeing her again. Squaring her shoulders, she began concentrating on her work.

Keeping busy was the one sure way to make the time pass faster until she saw him again. The feeling that he cared as deeply about her as she did for him made it seem easier somehow. There was strength to be drawn from that.

CHAPTER SEVEN

"MISTLETOE?" PERRY HELD UP the sprig by its red bow and cocked an eyebrow at Stephanie, kneeling in front of the fireplace to arrange the Nativity scene on its snowy blanket. "What on earth do we need mistletoe for in this house?"

"That's a good question." She sent him a teasing glance over her shoulder. "Maybe for that new schoolteacher, Miss Henderson. I understand she came into the restaurant for dinner again last night. I also understand that you just 'happened' to take your break at the same time."

"The restaurant was crowded," he defended himself, a redness spreading upward from his neck. "It seemed logical to ask her to sit at my table."

"But twice in half a week?" she mocked. "I didn't realize schoolteachers were paid the kind of wages that would allow them to eat at an expensive restaurant on Monday night and again on Wednesday. Or did she pay for her own meal both times?''

''Pattie really has a big mouth,'' Perry sighed in disgust.

And Stephanie laughed at the reference to the cashier, her source of information that had betrayed the fact that Perry had bought the young, attractive teacher's dinner the night before. ''Pattie is just worried about your single status.''

''It's none of her business.''

''Maybe not,'' she conceded. ''But in case you decide to invite Miss Henderson over for a glass of holiday cheer, why don't you hang the mistletoe from that center beam? It looks like a strategic location to me.''

''Who said I was going to invite her over?'' Perry bristled.

''Not me,'' Stephanie countered with wide-eyed innocence. ''But if you do, let me know. I can always spend the night at the inn.''

''Hang up your own mistletoe.'' Perry tossed it aside in ill humor and reached into the box of Christmas decorations to take out the wreath for the door.

''Get me the ladder and I will,'' she agreed, realizing that the new schoolteacher was an unusually touchy subject.

A sigh slipped from her lips as Perry stalked out of the room to fetch the ladder. She regretted ribbing him. It must be more than a casual flirtation for Perry to be so sensitive about it.

She certainly wasn't in any position to make light of someone else's relationship. She hadn't heard from Brock since Thanksgiving, which was two weeks ago. And two weeks could seem an eternity.

Perry returned with the ladder, not saying a word as he set it up beneath the beam where Stephanie had suggested that the mistletoe be hung. Leaving behind the smaller hammer, he took the heavier one and a couple of tacks, as well as the Christmas wreath of evergreen garlands, pinecones and red bows, and flipped on the outside light. He stepped outside and closed the door to keep the cold night air from chilling the living room.

Finished with the Nativity scene, Stephanie took the sprig of mistletoe, the hammer and a tack and climbed the ladder. One step short of the top she stopped and stretched to reach the hardwood beam.

Even though there was only the two of them, they traditionally hung their Christmas decorations after the tenth of December. The Christmas tree wasn't put up until the week before Christmas. Stephanie realized, a little ruefully, that neither of them was in the Christmas spirit on this night.

The phone started ringing before she had the mistletoe tacked into place. Stephanie hesitated, then continued to tap with the hammer, ignoring the commanding ring of the phone. The front door opened and Perry glared at her.

"Can't you hear the phone?" he snapped.

"That's only the third ring," she retorted just as impatiently.

"Fourth," he corrected, and walked briskly over to pick up the receiver and silence the irritating sound. "Hall residence," he answered with ill-tempered shortness, then paused. "Just a minute." He laid the receiver on the table with a thump. "It's for you."

The tack bent on the last strike of her hammer, which meant she had to start all over again with a new one. "Find out who it is and tell them I'll call back."

"I already know who it is—Brock." Just for a moment his expression softened. "Do you really want me to tell him you're too busy to talk right now?"

The mention of Brock's name sent her scrambling down the ladder, nearly upsetting it in her haste to get to the telephone. When she grabbed for the receiver, it slipped out of her fingers and crashed to the floor. Terrified she had broken it, Stephanie clutched it to her ear.

"Brock? Are you there?" Her voice was a thin thread of panic.

"My God, Stephanie! What did you do?" he demanded.

"I dropped the phone. I was on the ladder hanging the mistletoe when Perry answered the phone." She hurried her explanation. "I didn't realize you were the one who was calling until he told me. Then I was . . . ." It was too revealing to admit how excited she had been, so she changed her sentence. "I was in such a hurry to get to the phone that I became all thumbs."

"Are you glad I called?" His voice changed its texture, becoming warm and searching.

"You know I am," Stephanie murmured, and noticed her brother slipping out of the room so she could have some privacy. "It seems so long since I've heard your voice. I . . . ." She stopped, unable to actually admit the rest.

"You what, Stephanie? What were you going to say?" Brock insisted that she complete it. "Have you missed me?" He guessed her words.

"Yes, I've missed you." Her voice vibrated with the force of it.

"Why didn't you tell me that in your letters?" he demanded. "I couldn't stand it any longer, not knowing whether you were going through the same torment I've been suffering. The way you write, I get the feeling that everything is white and wonderful back there.''

"Have you really missed me, too?" She hardly dared to believe it was true.

"I've been out of my mind." An urgency entered his tone. "Stephanie, I have to see you. I can't wait any longer.''

"I want to see you, too." Her hand tightened on the telephone, trying to hold on to this moment. "C-can you come here?''

"No." He dismissed it as out of the question. "I'm in Palm Springs. I don't have a chance of getting away, not until around the holidays, *maybe*." He stressed the questionable status of that time. "I want you to come here, honey. I'll make all the arrangements. You can leave tomorrow morning and be here by noon. I'll only be able to spare a few hours in the afternoons to be with you over the weekend, but we'll have the nights—all of the nights.''

"Brock!" She was overwhelmed by the invitation and his determination to see her, whatever the cost.

"Don't worry about packing much or digging out your summer clothes. We'll go on a pre-Christmas shopping spree—just you and me.''

"You don't need to buy me anything," she interjected swiftly.

"I want to," he replied. "I wake up nights, thinking you're going to be lying beside me. I can't describe the hell I go through when you aren't there. Stephanie, will you come?"

A positive answer was on the tip of her tongue when she realized, "Brock, I can't." Disappointment throbbed in her voice, acute and painful.

"Why? What do you want me to do—beg?" He was angry and vaguely incredulous that she was refusing. "Why can't you come?"

"I have the payroll to finish. Tomorrow is payday for the employees at the inn," Stephanie explained.

"To hell with that! I want you here with me. Isn't that more important?" Brock argued. "Let someone else finish it."

"But there isn't anyone else who's qualified?"

"Your brother can do it. And don't tell me he doesn't know how," he retorted.

"He's overworked as it is, with the inn booked solid and temporary winter help. I couldn't do that." What Brock was asking was unreasonable and Stephanie tried to make him understand. "It isn't that I don't want to come, Brock. I can't."

"You can if you want to badly enough." Stubbornly he refused to listen to her explanations. "Tell everybody they'll have to wait until next week for the paycheck. I don't care. Stephanie, I've got to see you. I want you to fly here.''

"It's impossible. I can't do what you're asking. If you'd think about it, you would understand why.'' Her voice was growing tight with a mixture of anger and hurt confusion. "You aren't being fair.''

"Fair? The way I'm feeling isn't fair,'' Brock argued. "I need you.''

"Please don't do this.'' She was close to tears. "I can't come.''

There was a long silence before his voice returned grimly to the line. "All right, if that's the way you feel about it.''

"That isn't the way I feel. It's just the way it is,'' she choked.

"Have it your way.'' Brock sounded disinterested and very distant. "Goodbye.''

Stephanie sobbed in a breath as the line went dead. She stared numbly at the telephone for a long time before she finally wiped the tears from her cheeks. She was sniffling when Perry entered the room a short while later. He handed her his handkerchief, but didn't ask what was wrong.

He didn't say a word when she stuffed the mistletoe in the bottom of the box of Christmas decorations and carried the ladder out to the back porch. Her brother hadn't had any desire to hang it, and Stephanie thought it was highly unlikely that she would have a need for it.

IT WAS almost a week before she gathered the pride to write Brock a short note, saying only that she was sorry he hadn't understood her reason for turning down his invitation. But she subtly made it clear that she still believed she had made the right decision.

After writing that, she didn't write to him again. He had made it fairly plain that there wasn't any point. Perry had been a rock to her, never once reminding her that he had "told her so." Instead, he had tried to cheer her up each time her spirits sagged into the pits of despair—which was often.

They had weathered many depressing situations together. His support gave Stephanie the hope that she could do it again. Otherwise she wasn't certain what she would have done.

The week before Christmas their church had a Christmas caroling party. A skiing accident to one of the guests at the inn forced Perry to cancel at the last minute, but he encouraged Stephanie to go without him. Regarding it more as a religious festivity than a social party, she agreed.

He dropped her off at the church with instructions to call him when she was ready to go home and he would pick her up. It didn't prove necessary, however, since one of the first persons she met was Chris Berglund. His parents owned the farm a mile from theirs and the two had virtually grown up together—playmates becoming schoolmates. It had always seemed as though they were related, which they weren't.

Stephanie hadn't seen much of him since they had graduated from high school. Chris had gone on to college, coming back only for term breaks like this Christmas one.

When Chris learned she was without a lift home, he immediately volunteered to take her since it was right on his way to his parents. They gossiped, exchanged personal news and recalled funny incidents from their shared childhood days.

As he turned into the lane leading to the farmhouse, Stephanie leaned back in her seat and sighed. She couldn't remember when she had laughed like this and felt so lighthearted. She glanced at Chris, with his curly brown hair and dark-rimmed glasses, a thick parka adding bulk to his slim frame.

"I still can't believe you're going to be a doctor," she remarked. "I can remember when you used to squirm at the sight of blood."

"Thank heavens I outgrew that!" he laughed.

"Dr. Chris Berglund." Stephanie tried out the sound of the title with his name. "It has a very professional ring to it."

"It does, doesn't it?" he agreed with mock

smugness. "But I still have a few years of school left, plus my internship before that's a reality. I have to learn how to say 'Open your mouth and say, aah' with finesse!"

Stephanie laughed, as she was meant to do. "I'll bet your bedside manner will be impeccable."

"You know it." Chris slowed the car as he approached the house. "It looks like Perry is waiting up for you. Good grief, he even has the front light on for you. Is big brother playing the heavy-handed parent now?"

"That isn't his style. Perry is just Perry. I wouldn't trade him for the world," she replied, and meant it.

"He is a pretty special guy," Chris agreed, and stopped the car beside the shoveled sidewalk to the front door.

Stephanie climbed out of the car, joined by Chris as he walked around to see her to the door. "Why don't you come in for a drink?" she suggested. "Perry would love to see you."

"I'd better not." Chris turned down the invitation reluctantly. "I just got home this afternoon. With mom being in charge of the caroling party and all, I haven't got to visit much with the folks. The minister and his wife and a couple of mom and dad's friends are coming by the house tonight. I think they'd like to show me off."

"Naturally," Stephanie understood, stopping at the door and turning to him. "I'm glad you're home, Chris. It isn't the same when you aren't around."

"The next time I come, I'll bring a couple of guys from my fraternity. I'll fix you up with one of them," he winked. "I don't want my favorite girl turning into an old maid." He locked his hands behind her waist and pulled her closer. "You're much too pretty."

"Flatterer," she laughed, but there was a tight pain in her breast.

His kiss was a warm, friendly one, innocent and meaningless. It didn't occur to Stephanie to object—any more than it would have if a member of her family had kissed her. It was the same with Chris. Neither of them was hiding any secret passion for the other.

He was smiling when he drew away to leave. "Tell Perry I'll stop by the inn tomorrow. Maybe we can all have coffee together."

"Okay," she agreed, and added with a quick wave as he disappeared down the sidewalk, "Thanks for the ride!"

Her answer was a wave. Stephanie turned to enter the house as the car door slammed. Hurrying inside out of the cold, she paused to shut the front door and stomp the snow from her boots on the heavy mat inside.

"Hey, Perry!" she called to her brother as she turned and began unwinding the wool scarf from around her neck. "Guess who's home for Christmas?"

She had barely taken two steps into the living room when she saw a dark-coated figure standing beside the fireplace. She faltered in surprise before a searing joy ran through her veins.

"Brock!" she cried happily, and started forward with lighter steps.

"Surprise! Surprise!" Sarcasm dripped from his taunting voice, halting her as effectively as a barrier.

His left hand was thrust in the side pocket of his topcoat. In his right, he held a glass of whiskey. It had to be whiskey since that was the only kind of drink they kept in the house. His legs were slightly apart in a challenging stance. But it was the rawly bleak anger in his gray eyes that froze Stephanie. His masculine features might have been carved out of brown stone.

"When did you get here?" she managed finally. "Why didn't you let me know?"

"Fifteen minutes ago. What's the matter?" Brock jeered. "Are you wishing I'd come fifteen minutes from now so I wouldn't have witnessed that tender little scene out front?" His mouth thinned as he downed a swallow of whiskey. Angry disgust and contempt flared his nostrils.

"I'll bet you would have liked to know I was coming. You would have done a better job of juggling the men in your life so they wouldn't meet each other coming and going."

"Brock, that's not how it is," she protested in a pained voice.

"You mean that's not an example of how you wait for me?" he challenged with open scorn. "I saw you kiss him."

Stephanie half turned to glance at the glass pane on the top half of the front door, the outside light illuminating the entrance. If Chris had kissed her in the living room, they wouldn't have been more visible. Out of the corner of her eye she saw her brother appear in the kitchen opening, drawn by Brock's angry voice.

"It was Chris." She unconsciously appealed to her brother to make Brock understand how innocent the kiss had been.

"He's a neighbor—" Perry began, trying to come to her rescue.

"That's convenient," Brock snapped.

"You don't understand," Stephanie insisted helplessly.

"I understand all right." His voice was savagely low. "I understand that I was a fool to think you were different."

With unleashed fury he hurled the glass into the fireplace. Stephanie flinched at the crash of splintering glass and the subsequent small explosion of flames from the alcohol that splattered on the logs.

It all happened so quickly she didn't notice Brock was moving until he swept past her. By the time she turned, the front door was slamming in her face. She wrenched at the doorknob, the lock momentarily jamming from her haste.

She managed to jerk it open in time to see Brock striding around the station wagon to where his car was parked. The boxy bulk of that station wagon had previously hidden it from her view, but then she hadn't been looking for it, either.

As she ran down the sidewalk after Brock, she heard the car door slam and the motor start. Before she reached the driveway he had reversed onto the lane. Stephanie had a brief glimpse of his profile and the forbidding grimness of his expression before the car accelerated down the long drive.

"Stephanie?" Her brother was calling to her from the open front door.

She paused long enough to ask, "Are the keys in the wagon?"

"Yes. Where are you going?" he asked, already guessing.

"I've got to explain to him. I can't leave it like this." The answer was tossed over her shoulder as she ran to the car.

She lost sight of the Mercedes's taillights when she turned onto the main road. Judging by the direction Brock had taken, she took a chance that he was going to the inn.

His car was parked in the section reserved for employees, steam rising from the hood, when she arrived. She parked the station wagon beside it and hurried inside, slowing her steps to a fast walk through the lobby. Ignoring the questioning look she received from the night clerk, she didn't stop to explain what she was doing there at that hour of the night.

Her heart was pounding and she was out of breath when she reached the door to Brock's suite. Before she lost her nerve, she knocked rapidly three times. She felt a tense kind of relief when she heard hard strides approaching from the other side of the door. It was jerked open by an impatient hand. Brock's eyes narrowed on her with icy anger.

"I deserve the chance to explain what you saw," Stephanie rushed before he could order her to leave.

Minus his topcoat and suit jacket, he had on a white shirt, his tie askew from an attempt to loosen the knot. His hand returned to finish the job as he pivoted away from the door, not closing it. Stephanie moved hesitantly into the room, shutting the door behind her and watching the suppressed violence in the way he stripped the tie from around his neck and tossed it onto a seat cushion.

Without looking at her, he walked to the gold-leafed coromandel screen and opened it to reveal the bar. She watched him splash a couple of jiggers into a glass from a whiskey decanter. He took a quick swallow and moved away—not speaking, not looking at her.

"I . . . ." It was difficult to know how to begin when she was being so frigidly ignored. "Chris Berglund and I grew up together. We played as kids, we were in the same grade in school. He's studying to be a doctor and I haven't seen him in ages. He arrived home this afternoon for the Christmas break."

"You must have had a very joyous reunion," Brock remarked caustically.

"It was wonderful to see him again." Stephanie refused to deny that. "Chris and I are old friends. That's all we've ever been. It's more like we're brother and sister. I know how it might have looked—"

"Do you?" Brock spun around, withering her with the fiery blast of his anger. "Do you have any idea at all what it's like to break appointments, to tell important executives to go take a running jump into a lake, because there's this woman you can't get out of your head—and if you don't see her, you're likely to go crazy? So you take off, drop everything. Then you're there, in her home, waiting for her to come back from church— from *church*!" he emphasized with biting contempt. "You hear a car drive up and voices. You're so anxious to see her that you nearly go flying out the door. But there she is—kissing someone else."

"But it didn't mean anything." Her voice was hoarse, scraped by the rawness of the emotions he had displayed, his feeling of betrayal. "You've got to understand it was no different from kissing Perry."

"Am I supposed to believe that you missed me?" he challenged, unconvinced. "That you wanted to see me again?"

"Yes." She was astounded that he could doubt it.

"Then why haven't you written me?" Brock demanded, setting his glass down with a thump to punctuate the question.

"Because I thought . . . . When you called me and I couldn't come to California . . . ." Stephanie was so confused she couldn't finish one sentence before starting another. "You said goodbye . . . I thought it was final. You were angry because I refused," she reminded him.

"Yes." He began to cross the room. "I was furious—with you and with myself. When those letters stopped, I thought I'd lost you. I came all this way to apologize for being such a selfish, arrogant bastard." He stopped in front of her, reaching out to dig his fingers into the tender flesh of her shoulders. "Then, to find you in that man's arms, I . . . ."

The male lines in his face were more deeply etched as he struggled to control his warring emotions. With a smothered curse he crushed her lips beneath his, grinding them against her teeth. The brutality of his kiss bruised and punished, shocking Stephanie into the stillness of silent endurance until the moment of wrath passed.

Lifting his head to view her swollen and throbbing lips, Brock permitted her to breathe for a minute. Then his hands were forcing their way inside her parka and crushing her into his tortured embrace. Rough kisses were scattered over her hair and temples as anguished sounds moaned from his throat.

"Do you blame me for going a little crazy?" he groaned. "For wondering . . . ." He raised his head again, anger still smoldering in his eyes. "How many many men are there? How many men would fly halfway across the world to be with you?"

"Brock, there's only you," Stephanie whispered, lifting a trembling hand to let her fingertips trace the iron line of his jaw.

"That's what you say." Rueful cynicism flashed across his expression. "But I don't know what you do when I'm not here. My God, I don't even know if you're still a virgin!"

She was stunned that his doubt ran that deep. "You don't mean that!"

"Prove it," Brock challenged with a new urgency in his voice. His hands tightened their hold to draw her closer to the hardening contours of his body, making her vividly aware of his need. "Stay with me tonight."

"You expect me to go to bed with you just to prove I'm still a virgin," she accused, her hands straining against his chest to keep some distance between them. "What kind of a reason is that?"

"It's a damned good one!" he flared. "Because you're going to have to convince me that I haven't been going through this hell for nothing!"

"No!" A sudden surge of strength enabled her to wrench free of his arms and she backed quickly toward the door. "I shouldn't have to prove anything to you. Do I ask you how many women you've slept with since you met me? Don't forget I know about Helen! What kind of things do you think I imagine when you're gone? You can't have lain awake as many nights as I have wondering who you were with. But I promise you, tonight it isn't going to be me! Not for a reason like yours!''

Pivoting, she raced out the door into the hallway, but her haste was unnecessary. Brock made no attempt to follow her. The demons that pursued her were from her own imagination. She slowed her flight to walk swiftly through the lobby and outside to the station wagon.

A sense of justifiable indignation and pride kept her eyes dry and her chin steady. It wasn't until she was at home and alone in her bedroom that she began to think about some of the things Brock had said and the implications that he cared for her—even loved her.

Her temper cooled quickly when she realized she might have rejected the very thing she wanted most of all. The next question was whether she could swallow her pride and admit that to Brock.

CHAPTER EIGHT

ALL NIGHT LONG Stephanie wrestled with her dilemma. She awakened on Saturday morning no nearer to a solution than she had been the night before. Perry noticed the faint circles under her eyes at the breakfast table.

"How did it go last night? Did Brock listen to you?" He pushed his empty plate back and leaned on the table to finish his last cup of coffee.

"He listened." But she didn't say whether he had believed her.

"And?" her brother prompted.

"We argued," Stephanie admitted and rose from the table. "Do you want anything else before you leave?"

"No." He shook his head and downed the coffee. "It's late, I'd better be going. Are you going to wash clothes this morning? My basket of laundry is still in my room,'' he remarked on her change of routine. Usually she brought the dirty clothes downstairs before she fixed his breakfast.

''Yes . . . I'm going to wash. I'll get them later.'' At the moment, the laundry was the furthest thing from her mind. ''I'll see you tonight,'' she murmured absently.

After Perry had left, Stephanie decided to leave the laundry until later in the afternoon. Instead she chose to dust and clean the living room. Secretly she was hoping that Brock would make the first move to patch up their argument, so she didn't want to stay far from either the telephone or the front window.

The morning passed without a phone call, and she began to worry that Brock might have left. She couldn't stand the thought that they had parted on a bitter and angry note. Suddenly it seemed that she was being childishly stubborn by silently insisting that Brock had to be the first to say he was sorry they had argued.

She hurried to the phone and dialed the inn, asking to be connected to Brock's suite. Unconsciously she held her breath as she listened to his extension ring once, twice, three times, then—

''Yes?'' It was Brock. She recognized his voice instantly.

"It's Stephanie," she said, and waited for some kind of favorable reaction.

His response was a long time coming. Then it was a disappointing and noncommittal, "Yes?"

The telephone became a very impersonal and inadequate means of communication. "I'd like to talk to you. May I come and see you?" she requested, trying to be calm and not as anxious as she felt.

Again there was a pulse beat of silence. "When?"

"Now." Before she got cold feet.

Brock's pause was several seconds long. "I have some overseas calls I'm expecting. Perhaps later . . . say, about five o'clock," he suggested in a completely emotionless tone.

"That will be fine," she answered, because there was nothing else she could say.

"Good. I'll expect you then," he replied, clipped and to the point. "Goodbye."

"Yes . . . goodbye," Stephanie responded, then there was a click and the line was buzzing its dead signal in her ear. She slowly replaced the receiver, wondering if she had made the right decision after all by contacting him first. Brock couldn't have sounded more indifferent.

The dirty laundry was forgotten. Stephanie spent the afternoon taking a bath, washing and setting her hair, and trying on a half a dozen outfits before finally deciding on the rust-colored dress she had worn when she and Perry had dined with Brock and his blond companion that first day she had met him.

Without transportation since Perry had the station wagon, she had to call the local cab. Precisely at five o'clock she was standing in front of the door to Brock's suite. Mentally she rehearsed the speech she was going to make, then knocked on the door.

Brock opened it within seconds. There was a moment of silence as their eyes met. Stephanie thought she saw a flicker of something in the gray depths, but it was too quickly veiled for her to identify it. Her senses reacted to the coral silk shirt he was wearing, half-unbuttoned to give her an inviting glimpse of sun-browned skin and his dark chest hairs.

"You're right on time. Come in." A smile curved his mouth, but it lacked warmth.

"Thanks," she murmured as he stepped to one side to admit her. She nervously fingered the metal clasp of her purse, ill at ease with him and not understanding why.

His sharp gaze noticed the way she was fiddling with her purse. "Would you like a drink?" he suggested.

"Please." She felt in need of some kind of fortification. At the questioning lift of a male eyebrow, Stephanie added, "A whiskey and soda will be fine."

As Brock walked to the concealing gold-leafed screen, her gaze made a nervous sweep of the room. The room was immaculate. Except for his briefcase sitting on the floor near the phone, there wasn't any evidence that the sitting room had been used. The door to the bedroom was shut, but Stephanie suspected the same would be true in there.

Yet the atmosphere in the living room was teeming with invisible and dangerous undercurrents. She could feel them tugging at her.

Her gaze ran back to Brock, so aloof and so compelling. He had fixed two drinks, one for her and one for himself. Carrying them both, he crossed the room to hand Stephanie hers. The drink was not accompanied by an invitation to sit down and make herself comfortable.

Realizing that, she held the glass in both her hands and stared at the ice cubes floating in the amber liquid. She was rapidly beginning to regret coming to see him. She heard the ice clink in Brock's glass as he took a drink, but she knew her hands would start shaking if she lifted her glass.

"You said you wanted to see me," he reminded her.

"Yes." Stephanie lifted her gaze. "Last night

I was offended by some of the things you suggested," she began and searched his expression, hoping for perhaps a hint of remorse.

But his face was an impassive mask. She realized he had no intention of making this easier for her. The speech she had so carefully rehearsed was suddenly and completely forgotten.

Everything was thrown out as she made one last attempt to reach him. "If you want me to, I'll stay with you tonight. I love you, Brock."

Her confession didn't seem to make any impression on him. There wasn't even a flicker of an eyelash. "You'll get over it," was his cool response.

Stephanie couldn't believe that he could shrug it aside with that much disinterest. She stared at him, too stunned to hear the connecting door to the bedroom open. It was only when a voluptuous blonde in a see-through peignoir waltzed into her vision that she realized she and Brock weren't alone. It was Helen, the same girl Brock had been with the first time he had come.

"Darling—" she linked her arms around Brock's and pouted very prettily "—you promised we'd be alone for the rest of the evening."

"Stephanie, you remember Helen, don't you?" Brock drawled. Her gaze was transfixed by his mockingly cold smile. No color remained in her face. She was as white as one of his white leather chairs. "Fortunately Helen was able to join me for the weekend, otherwise I might have had to endure a night of amateur entertainment."

His taunting words rolled out to strike her. The glass slipped out of her numbed fingers, but she didn't hear it crash to the floor. She reeled from the stinging blow, turning to rush blindly from the room. Hot tears rolled down her cheeks in an avalanche of pain.

Shame and humiliation consumed her with a burning heat. Conscious only of the desperate need to escape, she wasn't aware of the stares or turning heads as she ran through the lobby and out through the front door.

Not even the zero temperature cooled the scalding heat of her pain. Sobbing, she realized she had no place to run, except home. The station wagon was parked to one side in front of the entrance. Hurrying to it, she glanced inside and had to wipe the tears away before she could see the keys dangling out of the ignition.

Climbing behind the wheel, she started the engine and reversed out of the parking space. The tears refused to stop falling, now that the deluge had begun. As she turned onto the main road, she nearly sideswiped an incoming car, swinging the wheel to avoid it just in time.

Shrugging free of Helen's hold, Brock walked over and shut the door Stephanie had left open.

His shoes crunched on the broken glass around the liquor stain on the floor. He gulped a swig of his own drink, trying to wash down the bad taste in his mouth. His gaze flicked uninterestedly to the near-naked girl.

"The show is over. Put a robe on, Helen," he ordered in a flat voice.

Her gaze swept him with a disapproving look. With a swirl of gauzy nylon, she disappeared inside the bedroom. He finished the rest of his drink and waited for its deadening effect to begin. It didn't work with its usual swiftness and he walked to the bar to refill his glass.

He walked away, carrying the decanter of whiskey as well as his glass. Stretching his long frame in a chair, his legs spread in front of him, he stared broodingly out the window at the snow-covered mountains.

He barely glanced up when Helen returned, covered from neck to ankle in an ermine-trimmed robe of black. It was a perfect foil to her perfectly bleached platinum hair. Without waiting for him to suggest it, she walked to the bar and poured herself a gin and tonic.

"Do you want me to call a maid to clean up this mess?" she asked, gesturing toward the broken glass and the spreading pool of liquid.

"No." Brock shut his eyes. His lungs felt as if they were about to burst.

"Did you have to be so rough on her?" Helen complained. "Couldn't you have let her down with a little more class?"

"It was the best way I knew to be sure she got the message." He heard the weariness in his voice, the utter fatigue.

"There are times when I'm not sure that you have a heart, Brock Canfield," she retorted.

"There's such a thing as being cruel to be kind." He lifted his glass and studied its contents in the waning light of the winter afternoon. "I'm not the four-bedroom type."

A WALL OF tears blocked Stephanie's vision. She couldn't see where she was going or even if she was driving on the road. It had ceased to matter. When the station wagon began to skid on the slippery road, she stopped trying to control it and let it go wherever it wanted. It spun and bumped, coming to an abrupt halt. The suddenness of it catapulted her forward against the steering wheel.

It didn't occur to her that she had had an accident. She simply took advantage of the steering wheel's support, folding her arms to rest her forehead against them and cry. There was an ocean of pain dammed up behind her eyes. Tears seemed the only way to relieve the unbearable pressure.

"ARE YOU PLANNING to get drunk, Brock?" Helen questioned from her reclining position on the sofa. "Or is that whiskey decanter you're holding just a security blanket?"

Brock glanced at the crystal decanter with its glass stopper in place and his empty glass that hadn't been refilled. "I'm considering it."

But it didn't seem worth the effort. The stupor would eventually wear off and he'd be back to square one. A knock at the door tipped his head back as he lifted a hand to cover his eyes.

"Answer that," he told Helen. "Send whoever it is away. I don't want to see anyone."

With a soft rustle of material, the girl swung her legs off the sofa to rise and walk to the door in her satin mules. She opened the door with a secretive little flourish. "I'm sorry, but Mr. Canfield can't see anyone just now," she murmured coyly.

"He'll see me." Perry Hall pushed his way into the suite.

"Oh, dear, Brock, it's the brother," Helen declared in mock dismay.

Brock let his hand drop to the armrest. He could do without a confrontation with Stephanie's brother, but he had been expecting it. "What do you want, Perry?" he sighed.

"I want to know where Stephanie's gone." He stopped in front of Brock's chair, square jawed and stern.

"How should I know?" His gaze narrowed faintly. "She isn't here."

"But she was here. And I'm betting that *she*—" Perry gestured toward Helen "—is the reason Stephanie ran out of here crying."

"That's a question you'll have to put to Stephanie." Brock unstoppered the decanter and filled his glass.

"When I find her," Perry replied. "She drove off in my station wagon."

"Then she probably went home," Brock shrugged.

"She didn't. I've called and called, but there wasn't any answer. Finally I got hold of our neighbors. They went over to the house, but she wasn't there."

The announcement rolled Brock to his feet. "Are you saying that she's missing?" The demand came out as a smooth question.

"Yes. I don't know what happened here or what was said, but I do know the kind of state Stephanie was in when she ran out of the lobby," Perry retorted. "And she wasn't in any condition to be driving. Since you were responsible, you

owe me the loan of your car so I can go and look
for her.''

"I'll get the keys." Brock walked into the
bedroom and came out wearing his parka. "I'm
coming with you."

"I don't need you along," her brother rejected
his offer.

"I'm not asking your permission." Brock
moved toward the door. "Since, as you say, I'm
responsible for your sister's overwrought condition, I'm going along to make certain she's all
right."

"You should have thought about that before,"
Perry accused.

"I'm aware of my past mistakes," Brock
countered. "What happened today will ultimately
turn out for Stephanie's own good. You and I
both know that, Perry."

"I warned her that you would hurt her, but she
wouldn't listen," Perry sighed.

"I didn't hurt her as much as I could have."

STEPHANIE FELT DRAINED and empty, without the
strength to even lift her head. Her throat was dry
and aching, scraped raw by the last sobs. Her
eyes burned with aridness. There wasn't even
any relief when she closed them. She hurt; she
hadn't realized it was possible to hurt so badly
that being alive was agony.

There was a noise, then an influx of fresh, cold air, but she didn't welcome its reviving attempt. Something gripped her shoulders. A voice called her name. It sounded so much like Brock's that Stephanie was convinced she was dreaming. She moaned in protest when she was gently pulled away from the support of the steering wheel and forced to rest against the back of the seat.

"Are you hurt, Stephanie?" It still sounded like Brock. "Can you hear me?"

"Yes," she rasped thinly, but didn't bother to open her eyes. None of this was real, anyway.

The familiar and caressing gentleness of Brock's hands was exploring her face, smoothing the hair away from her forehead. The sensation was sweet torment.

"I can't find any sign of a cut or a bruise." It was Brock's voice again, low and concerned.

"Stephanie, do you remember what happened?"

The second voice made her frown. It belonged to her brother. "Perry?" Mustering her strength, she opened her eyes.

Again there was a sensation of being in a dream. Brock was half-sitting on the driver's seat and facing her. A deep furrow ran across his forehead, pulling his eyebrows together. She felt weepy again, but there weren't any tears left. Something made her glance sideways. There was Perry, bending low and trying to crowd into the car.

"I'm here, Stephanie," her brother assured her. "Do you remember what happened? How long have you been here?"

"I don't . . . know." The last question she could answer, but the first meant pain. Stephanie looked back at Brock. None of it was a dream. She knew exactly where she was and why. She pushed his hand away from her face. "Why are you here? You should be back at the suite being entertained by your sexy friend," she accused in a breaking voice. "Go away and leave me alone!"

But he ignored her. "Did you hit your head when the car spun into this snowdrift?" His hand went back to her head, feeling for bumps on her scalp.

"No, no, I wasn't hurt at all," she insisted huskily, and pushed his hand away again. "I lost control of the car—on a patch of ice, I guess. Is that what stopped me—a snowbank?"

"You're lucky it wasn't a telephone pole," Brock muttered and reached for her arm. "Come on, let's get you out of the car."

"No!" Stephanie eluded his hand and turned to her brother. "I want to go home, Perry," she said tightly, edging along the seat to the passenger side.

She had a glimpse of her reflection in the rear view mirror. Her face was pale and colorless, her eyes swollen and red from the tears, and her cheeks stained with their flow. She looked like a washed-out mop. It wasn't fair that Brock had seen her this way.

She hadn't wanted to give him the satisfaction of knowing how his callousness had crushed her. That was why she had run. She stared at her hands, twisting white in her lap as Brock stepped away from the driver's side to let her brother slide behind the wheel.

After he had started the motor, he shifted the car into reverse. The tires spun, then found some traction and they were bouncing backward out of the hard-packed snow. Brock stood by the roadside, his hands in his pockets, watching them. For a moment he was outlined there, alone, his gaze lingering on her. Then the station wagon was moving forward.

"Why did you have to bring him along with you?" Stephanie choked painfully on the question, her eyes misting with tears again.

"It was his car. He insisted." His gaze left the road, swinging to her. "Are you okay?"

"No, I don't think so." She stared sightlessly out of the window at the bleak landscape of snow and barren trees. "All those lines always sounded so melodramatic before—but, Perry, I wish I could die.''

When they reached the house, Stephanie went directly to her room. Without changing clothes or turning on a light, she lay down on her bed, huddling in a tight ball atop the covers. It was nearly nine when Perry knocked on her door and entered the room carrying a tray with a bowl of hot soup and crackers.

"Go away, please," she requested in a flat voice.

Setting the tray on the bedside table, he switched on the lamp. "You have to eat, Stephanie."

"No." She rolled away into the shadows on the opposite side of the bed.

"Just a little, Stephanie," he insisted in that patient voice of his. She rolled back and he smiled gently. "Sit up." He fixed the pillows to prop her up and set the tray on her lap. For his sake, she ate a few spoonfuls, but it had no taste for her. When she handed it back to him, Perry didn't attempt to coax her into eating more.

It was nearly midnight before she roused herself sufficiently out of her stupor to change into her nightdress and crawl beneath the covers. She didn't sleep, at least not the kind of sleep she normally knew.

With dull eyes, she watched the dawn creep into her bedroom through the east window. She heard the church bells ring their call to early service, but didn't leave her bed to respond to them. Perry came in with orange juice, coffee and toast. She sampled a little of each of them . . . for him.

All morning she stayed in her room. When Perry came to tell her he was going to the inn for an hour or so, Stephanie merely nodded. She heard him come home in the middle of the afternoon, but she didn't leave her bedroom.

At the supper hour, Perry came in. "The food's on the table."

"I'm not hungry." She sat in the center of her bed, hugging her pillow.

"Stephanie, you can't stay in this room forever," he pointed out. "It was rough. It hurt like hell, I know. But it's over. You've got to pick up the pieces and start again." She stared at him, hearing this truth that was so difficult to put into practice. "Come on." He offered his hand. "The longer you stay here, the harder it will be to leave."

Hesitantly, she placed her hand in his and let him help her off the bed. Together they went downstairs to the kitchen. She sat down at the table with its platter of Yankee pot roast, potatoes, onions and carrots. The irony of it stabbed her as she remembered Brock had said she was pot roast while he was Chateaubriand.

"Has . . . has Brock left?" she faltered on the question.

The carving knife was poised above the meat as Perry shot a quick glance at her. "Yes."

A violent shudder quaked through her, but she made no sound.

THE NEXT MORNING she was up before Perry. She discovered that routine was something solid to cling to in her shattered world. She made coffee, got their breakfast, dressed and drove to the inn with Perry. There was one difference. She closed her office door when she went to work. She was no longer interested in the comings and goings of the inn's guests.

There were questions, kindly meant, from her fellow workers, but she turned them aside. She knew they were making their own guesses about what might have transpired, but she didn't offer them any information that would fuel more gossip.

All around her were the festive decorations of Christmas, cheerful voices calling holiday greetings, and the merry songs of the season drifting through the halls. This time, no spirit of glad tidings lightened her heart.

Chris Berglund came over several times while he was home for the holidays. Stephanie suspected the frequency of his visits was at her brother's instigation. But mostly he talked to Perry while she made certain there was plenty of cocoa, coffee or beer for the two of them to drink. She appreciated that Perry was trying to keep the time from stretching so emptily. In a way his methods worked.

The coming of the new year brought changes. Stephanie's appetite was almost nonexistent. She ate meals because they were necessary, but she lost weight. She rarely slept the whole night through. In consequence, there was a haunting look to her blue eyes, mysterious and sad. She rarely smiled and laughed even less frequently. Her chestnut hair was worn pulled away from her face, secured in a neat coil. The style was very flattering and sophisticated, adding to her touch-me-not air.

Unless she was escorted by Perry, Stephanie didn't attend any social function. Even long-time friends saw little of her. Except to shop or go to the inn to work, she rarely left the farmhouse.

New Hampshire natives clucked their tongues when she walked down the streets, prophesying that she would surely become an old maid. With Perry seeing more and more of the young schoolteacher, they wondered among themselves what she would do if her brother got married.

But Stephanie couldn't look ahead any further

than the next day. It was the way she had got
through January, February and March. It hadn't
been easy. She wondered if it ever would. But
the worst was over . . . over.

CHAPTER NINE

PRECARIOUSLY BALANCED on a metal folding chair, Stephanie reached as far as she could, but she still couldn't reach the square of dust taunting her from the rear top of the filing cabinet. Sighing, she straightened to stand on the unsteady chair.

The door to her office opened and Perry entered. "Hi."

Affection warmed her eyes, although the curve to her lips was barely discernible. "Hi, yourself. Your timing is excellent." She carefully stepped down from the chair. "I need your long arm to dust the back of the cabinet."

"What's this? Spring-cleaning time?" Good-naturedly, he took the duster she handed him and stepped onto the chair, easily reaching the rear of the metal top.

"It's the right time of year," Stephanie pointed

out. The calendar on the wall was opened to April. "Besides, I didn't have anything else to do this afternoon."

"Mud season is always the slow time of year," he joked. "Want me to dust the top of the other cabinet?"

"As long as you're here, be my guest." Taking a spare duster, she started toward the metal storage cabinet where the extra stationery and forms were kept. The shelves looked as if someone had been finger painting in the dust.

"Brock's coming," said Perry.

She had lived in dread of those words. They hit her, spinning her around toward Perry. Accidentally she knocked the wooden cylinder filled with pens and pencils off her desk, scattering them on the foor.

"Damn!" She choked out the word and bent hurriedly to pick them up, grateful for a reason to hide the tears that sprang into her eyes.

She had forced the tears all inside by the time she had gathered all the pencils. Her hands were shaking when she returned the cylinder to the desk. Perry was feigning interest in the sharpness of her letter opener, giving her a chance to recover.

"When. . .?" She had to swallow the lump in her throat and try again. "When is he coming?"

"This weekend. On Friday," he tacked on to be more specific.

"Oh." The duster was twisted into a tight ball in her hands.

"Are you going to run and hide?" His question was really a challenge.

It made her feel like a first-class coward, because it was exactly what she wanted to do. "No." But it was a very small sound.

"Good girl," her brother praised. She lifted her head, letting him see the tortured anguish in her eyes. "Come on," he cajoled, "let's see some of that stiff New England backbone."

"Sure." She took a deep breath and turned away.

He clamped a hand on her shoulder in a firm display of affection. "There isn't much happening around here today. We'll leave early this afternoon, around four, okay?"

"Do you have a date tonight with Joyce?" she asked, trying to follow his change of subject.

"No, not tonight. See you later." He moved toward the door.

Stephanie walked back to her desk and sat down. Brock was coming. It twisted her inside until she wanted to cry out, but she didn't. She had been bracing herself for this moment. Now it had come—her first true test. After nearly four months, surely she would survive it.

FRIDAY. FRIDAY. FRIDAY. Each beat of her pulse seemed to hammer out the word. When she arrived at the inn that morning she was a nervous wreck, despite her well-disciplined outward show of calm.

It took her twice as long as usual to get the payroll checks ready for Perry's signature. Especially the last few, because that was when Perry stuck his head in the door to tell her Brock had just driven up. After that, she mentally jumped at nearly every sound, expecting him to walk in.

She skipped lunch to finish payroll, finally getting it done at two o'clock. Gathering them into a folder, she walked down the hall to Perry's office. The door was standing open, but he wasn't there.

Probably with Brock, Stephanie surmised and walked in to leave the folder on his desk. Out of habit, she paused to straighten the leather desk set that had belonged to their father.

"Excuse me, miss." Brock's voice ran through her like a lightning bolt. "Could you tell me where I could find Mr. Hall?"

It gradually dawned on her that the question was being addressed to her. She turned slowly to see him framed by the doorway. Tall, dressed in a gray suit, he was every bit as compelling as she remembered him, if not more so. She watched the disbelief of recognition flash across his expression.

"Stephanie," he murmured her name and took a step into the office. "You've changed. I didn't recognize you."

His gray eyes seemed to examine every detail from her willowy figure to the new, sophisticated way she wore her hair. His inspection left the sensation that he had physically touched her. Inside, she was a quaking mass of nerves.

"Yes, I've changed," she admitted, but not where he was concerned. The love she felt was just as strong, if not tempered by the separation. She turned away, pretending to straighten some papers to keep from giving in to the impulse to throw herself into his arms. "I'm afraid I don't know where my brother is. Perhaps you should check at the desk."

"How are you?" Brock inquired, his voice coming from only a few feet behind.

"I'm fine." That was a lie. She was dying inside. But she turned to face him and lend strength to her assertion.

At closer quarters she could see the changes times had made on him. Still vital, still vigorously masculine, he looked leaner in the face. The hollows of his cheeks were almost gaunt. More lines were carved into his skin or else previous ones had grown deeper, especially around his eyes, where they fanned out. And he seemed harder.

"From all the reports I received, the inn did exceptionally good winter business," he remarked.

"Yes. It seems quite empty now, but spring is generally slow." Why was she letting this conversation continue? Why didn't she leave? Stephanie was angry with herself for not possessing the willpower to walk out the door. With a defiant tilt of her chin, she flashed him a cold look. "But I'm sure that won't bother you, since you bring your entertainment with you." Then she was angry for referring even indirectly to his female companions. "Excuse me, I have work to do."

She brushed past him, hurrying from the room before she made a complete fool of herself. She met Perry in the hall.

"Brock's looking for you. He's in your office." Her voice was brittle with the force of her control.

Concern flashed quickly. "Are you okay?"

Her answer was a silent, affirmative nod. He touched her arm as he walked by her to his office. Stephanie slipped quickly into her own and leaned against the door, shaking in reaction. It was several minutes before her legs felt strong enough to carry her to the desk.

At five o'clock Perry came to take her home. As they drove away from the inn, he said, "You don't have to worry about getting dinner tonight."

"I suppose you're eating out tonight." *With Brock,* she added silently.

"You're half-right," he replied cheerfully, and she realized he had been in a good mood when he picked her up. "*We* are eating out tonight."

"Perry, I—" Stephanie started to refuse.

"It's in the way of a celebration," he inserted, and glanced at her. When he saw the look in her eyes, he smiled. "Brock isn't going to be there. At least, he isn't invited." Her brother actually laughed. "Just you, me and Joyce. She's meeting us at the inn."

Celebration. Joyce, the schoolteacher. "Are. . . ?" There was a quick rush of gladness at the implication. Stephanie turned in her seat, her eyes wide and shining. "Perry, are you and Joyce getting married? Are we celebrating your engagement?"

"That isn't exactly what we're celebrating, at least not yet," he hedged. "I haven't even asked her yet. Do you like her, Stephanie?"

"Yes, and I rather fancy the idea of having her for a sister-in-law," she admitted. "But let's get back to this dinner. What are we celebrating tonight if it isn't your engagement?"

"That's a surprise. I'm saving it for dinner," Perry declared with a secretive complacency. "And you haven't got all night to dress. I promised Joyce we'd meet her a little after six, so you have to hustle."

One other change her weight loss had made besides slenderizing her appearance was that her closet was filled with a whole new wardrobe. It wasn't nearly as difficult to chose what to wear since Stephanie liked them all. In view of Perry's insistence that tonight's dinner was a celebration, she picked an aquamarine dress of whipped silk.

Joyce Henderson was waiting for them when they returned to the inn. A petite and pert brunette, she was naturally outgoing and intelligent. Stephanie thought she was a perfect choice for her brother, who tended to be too serious at times.

"What's this all about, Perry?" Joyce questioned immediately. "You were so mysterious about it on the phone this afternoon."

"Just wait," he insisted, taking her arm and guiding her to the restaurant entrance.

"Has he told you, Stephanie?" She looked around Perry's bulk at Stephanie.

"He hasn't given me as much as a hint," she replied.

"You'll both find out soon," he promised. After they were seated at a table, he waved aside the dinner menus. "We'll order later. Bring us a bottle of champagne."

"Champagne?" Stephanie frowned. "You really meant it when you said this was going to be a celebration! How much longer are you going to keep us in suspense?"

"Wait for the champagne." Her brother was enjoying the secrecy.

The champagne arrived. Because the waiter was serving his boss, there was a little extra pomp and ceremony attached to popping the cork and pouring a sample for his approval. Finally the three glasses were filled with the sparkling wine.

"All right, the champagne is here. Now out with it," Joyce demanded.

Perry lifted his glass and started to speak, but his gaze focused on a point to the left of Stephanie, then ran swiftly to her. It was the only warning she received before Brock spoke.

"I find myself dining alone this evening. Do you mind if I join you?" he asked.

They were seated at a table for four, and the chair that was vacant was next to Stephanie. She wanted to cry out to Perry to refuse permission, but her voice failed her. Or perhaps she knew Perry wouldn't listen to her, anyway.

"Of course, Brock. Sit down," her brother invited with subdued enthusiasm and motioned to the waiter to bring another place setting.

Stephanie sat silently through Perry's introduction of Joyce to Brock, aware of the dark-suited shoulder and arm next to her. But she wouldn't look at him. She couldn't look at him.

It didn't seem to matter. Her senses were filled with his presence—the vigorously male smell of his cologne, the warm, rich sound of his voice and the sensation that she only had to reach out to touch him.

Another glass of champagne was poured for Brock. "Have you told them the news?" he asked Perry.

"Not yet," he admitted.

"You know what it is?" Stephanie sent Brock a surprised look and her gaze was caught by the enigmatical grayness of his.

He held it for an enchanted instant, then his gaze slid to Perry. "I know about it."

"Will one of you tell us?" Joyce suggested with faint exasperation.

Perry hesitated, bouncing a glance at Stephanie. "Brock is selling the inn."

"That doesn't come as a surprise." Although it was possibly a cause for celebration even if she didn't feel it at the moment. She fingered the stem of her wineglass, darting a look in Brock's direction. "The inn was really a nuisance to you, anyway. I'm sure you'll be glad to get it off your hands."

"I will, but not for your reason," Brock replied, but didn't explain what his reason was.

"Is this what we're celebrating?" Joyce was confused.

Perry glanced at her and smiled. "He's selling it to me. You're sitting with the future owner of the White Boar Inn."

"What? I don't believe it!" Joyce was incredulous and ecstatic at the same time. She was laughing while tears glittered in her eyes. "Perry, that's wonderful!"

"I think so," he agreed.

"I'm glad for you," Stephanie offered. For herself, she knew how much she would miss the previous owner.

But her brother didn't seem to notice her lukewarm congratulations as glasses were raised in a toast. Stephanie barely sipped at her champagne, not needing its heady effects when Brock was sitting beside her, disrupting her composure and destroying her calm.

"Perry didn't explain the proposal I offered him," said Brock, glancing at Stephanie over the rim of his glass. "Actually I gave him two choices."

"Yes, well, I made my choice," her brother shrugged. "It's what I really want. There isn't any question in my mind."

"What was the other choice?" Stephanie glanced from her brother to Brock. She sensed there was something significant here.

"I explained to him this afternoon that I'd decided to sell the inn," Brock began. "If he wanted to buy it, I agreed to personally finance it for him or . . ." he paused, "I offered to give him a full year's pay plus a bonus—more than enough to pay his tuition through law school."

"But . . . ." She stared at her brother. "I don't understand. . . ."

"Neither did I, until Brock offered me the choice." He shook his head, as if a little amazed by it himself. "But when it was there in front of me, I knew that what I really wanted was this place. All my life I thought I wanted to be a lawyer, but when it came right down to it, I couldn't give up this place."

"I know the feeling," said Brock. "The inn isn't the only thing I'm selling. Quite a few of my other companies are on the market. And I'm consolidating the rest of my holdings.'' He set his wineglass down, watching the bubbles rise to the surface. ''As a matter of fact, I'm looking at some four-bedroom homes.''

Stephanie's heart stopped beating. She was afraid to breathe or move, terrified that she was reading something into that statement that Brock didn't mean. Her wide blue eyes stared at him. Slowly he lifted his gaze to look at her.

''Would you be interested in helping me pick one out, Stephanie?'' he asked huskily. ''I don't want there to be any question about my intentions, so I'm asking you in front of your brother—will you marry me?''

''Yes.'' Where was her pride? Quickly Stephanie retracted it. ''No.'' Then she wavered, ''I don't know.''

''You need a more private place than this to convince her, Brock,'' Perry suggested.

''Will you let me convince you?'' He studied her.

''Yes,'' she whispered.

''Excuse us.'' Brock rose from his chair and waited for her to join him.

She felt like a sleepwalker lost in a marvelous dream as Brock escorted her from the restaurant, his hand lightly resting on the small of her back, faintly possessive. She stiffened in mute resistance when she realized he was guiding her to his suite.

It was the scene of too many conflicting and

painful memories. Anywhere else and she might have melted right into his arms the minute they were alone. But when he closed the door, she put distance between them.

"Why, Brock? Why, after all this time?" she asked, remembering the days of hell she'd been through.

"Because I made the same discovery Perry did. I always thought I had the way of life I wanted, until I met you. Even then I didn't recognize what was happening. I didn't see the choice that was in front of me. In these last few months I've had my way of life, but I finally realized that it could all go down the drainpipe and I wouldn't care, if I had you."

"But—" Stephanie turned, searching his face, wanting desperately to believe him "—here . . . Helen . . . ." It was such a painful memory that she couldn't put it into words.

"I know how much I hurt you." A muscle flexed in his jaw as he clenched it. "I wanted you from the moment I met you. I fooled myself into believing we could have an affair—a long affair—even later I thought our marriage could survive my life-style," he said. "Then that night when I made a jealous idiot of myself over that neighbor of yours, and you pointed out the uncertainties and torment you felt when I was away, I knew that constant separations would ultimately kill what we had. I was being ripped apart by them already. I can only imagine what you were going through.''

"Why didn't you explain that?'' she questioned, aware that he was moving toward her.

"Because, my lovely Yankee, we might have convinced each other we could make it work. So when you called asking to see me, I knew you were coming with the intention of making up. I put you off and called Helen in Boston.'' His hands began to move in a series of restless caresses over her shoulders. "I wanted you so much I couldn't trust myself alone with you—I couldn't trust myself to resist your possible arguments. So I staged that scene with Helen, arranged for her to walk in within minutes after you arrived.''

"How could you?'' It was a tautly whispered accusation, ripe with remembered pain.

"It was cruelly vicious, I admit it.'' His eyes glittered with profound regret. "But I never for one minute thought that one of the first things you would say was that you loved me. The hardest thing I've ever done was reject you and your love. I thought it might be easier for you if I made you hate me.''

"You nearly succeeded!''

"Nearly?'' He cupped her chin in his hand and raised it to study her face. "You mean you don't hate me.''

"No. Brock, I love you. I've never stopped loving you,'' Stephanie admitted.

His arm curved her slender form to the muscular hardness of his body as he bent his head to seek her lips, parting them hungrily, needing her as desperately and completely as she needed him. Love flamed wild and glorious, sweeping them up in its radiant heat. Breathing shakily, Brock lifted his head before the embrace turned into an inferno.

"Why did you wait so long?" Stephanie sighed.

"Because nobody was there to offer me a clear-cut choice—you or the Canfield legacy. I was too much of a fool to realize it was that simple. But you can believe this." He framed her face in his hands, gazing at it as if it was the loveliest work of art in the world. "I love you, Stephanie. And I don't care if I never have another glass of champagne, sleep in another hotel suite or eat Chateaubriand for the rest of my life."

"I never thought I'd be this happy again," she confessed, beaming with the joy filling her heart.

"Everything I said tonight—about selling and consolidating, you realize that it can't happen overnight," Brock cautioned. "It'll take at least a year. In the meantime I'll still have to travel a lot. After that, it will only be a few times a year. Then you can come with me."

"Whatever you say," Stephanie murmured.

"Just let me love you, let me make up for all the pain I've caused you." His mouth moved onto hers, gently at first, then with increasing ardor. Long minutes passed before either of them recovered sufficient control of their senses to come up for air. "How much time will your brother need to find a new bookkeeper so I can marry my bride?"

"This is the slack season." She smoothed her hand over his richly dark hair, enjoying the feel of its thickness against her fingers. "And I do have some influence with the boss. Maybe a week, two at the most."

"Where would you like to spend your honeymoon? The Caribbean? The Virgin Islands maybe?" he taunted affectionately. "What about Europe? Or maybe right here in the honeymoon suite where it all started?"

"Here." Stephanie didn't even hesitate over the choice.

"I think I'll arrange to have that king-sized bed replaced." His hands familiarly tested the slimness of her build. "I could lose you in that."

"Think so?" She brushed her lips across the corner of his mouth.

"I'm not going to take the chance," Brock murmured before he fastened his mouth onto her teasing lips in a kiss that branded her forever his.